THE
PSI.P.O.

KENNETH ROLAND

Build: 1.0.9
Copyright © 2021 Kenneth Roland
All rights reserved.
Layout design © 2021 Rebaken Enterprises
Published 2021 by Rebaken Enterprises
ISBN: 978-1-7779137-0-0
Cover design by K. J. Roland
Liquid Crystal Font by Chase Babb

Though some of the places and buildings mentioned in The Psi.P.O. are real, all events and characters are the products of the author's imagination. Any resemblence to real persons, alive or dead, is entirely coincidental. No part of this book may be reproduced or transmitted in any form or by any means, electronic or mechanical, including photocopying, recording, or by any information storage and retrieval system, without the author's permission.

To my grandfather, who never stopped making things.

*To my surrogate father, Jerry Keenan,
from the son he never wanted.*

*To my mom and dad for surviving
those years I was smaller than them.*

To my poor suffering wife Rebecca, the foundation of my life.

*To my four girls, Hannah, Kennedy, Madison & Alex.
Without you, I wouldn't know what drama was.*

To K. J. Roland, a truly great man.

*To Bunny & Jamie for being the type of friends you can
call anytime and know they will support you in anything.*

*To Kathy and Bill, my siblings, who have spent their entires lives
with me, they are the real heroes.*

*To Sean Alderdice for inspiring me to read back when
I just wanted to party.*

To Mr. MacDonald, my eigth grade teacher.

*To Rebaken Enterprises for letting me
put as many dedications as I want*

*And especially to you, the reader that
made it this far down the page. Thank you.*

ACKNOWLEDGEMENTS

The author would like to aknowledge the following persons and groups for their help with this story. Thanks to my proof readers: Rebecca Roland, John Dickinson, Harry Scanlan, Bill Roland, Andy Heller, and Dinah Davis.

Please check out Code Like A Girl
https://code.likeagirl.io/
Code Like A Girl is a space that celebrates women in technology. They hope to achieve this by amplifying the voices of women and their allies.

Thanks to Andy Heller for suggesting that books should never be judged by their contents.

Special thanks to Chris Stavropoulos for collecting the largest bug bounty of typos and errors.

A huge thanks to my co-workers that make every day a joy.

The story you are about to read is fiction. Any resemblence to a real story is strictly coincidental. The story, all names, characters, and incidents portrayed are completely fictitious. The names of all characters have been changed even though they were just made up to begin with, and then changed again just to be safe.

Dataffair HR Report

MEATSTICKS PLEASE!!!

Last Name	First Name	Position	Years
Joffrey	Malcolm	Co-Founder	2
Cliff	Gillian	Co-Founder	2
Reynolds	Matthew	Architect	1.5
Kennedy	Nasser	Software Developer	1.5
Khatri	Rajesh	Software Developer	1.5
Ziraldo	Michael	Software Developer	2
Bates	James	Software Tools	1
Singh	Sachet	Quality Assurance	1
Westfield	Daniel	Software Developer	.5
Miller	Andrea	User Experience	.5
LaFontaine	Cheryl	Everything Else	.5
Johnston	Brad	Information Tech.	.25
Gibbons	Stephen	Security Engineer	.25
Gupta	Neeru	Security Engineer	.25
Hartley	Alex	Software Developer	.25

Open Positions: Vice President of Sales
Bookkeeper

Congratulations On Initial Launch - Cake

Photo courtesy photos-public-domain.com

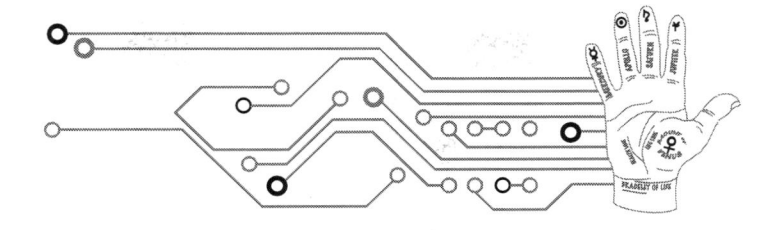

CHAPTER 0000 0000: THE UPSIDE OF STARTING

"What do you mean we have no logo?" Malcolm stared at Andrea in disbelief. "I thought we ran that contest weeks ago, everyone was supposed to submit their ideas and we were going to pick the best ... remember?"

"Yes. I remember very clearly giving you and Gillian those logo ideas and you said you'd tell me the winner last week." answered Andrea, throwing her hands up in exasperation.

"Oh for crap." muttered Malcolm, remembering being given those print-outs and putting them somewhere safe, that he will never remember again. "OK, let's see them, I'll just pick one and we can run with it to start, we can change it later."

Andrea sighed. "Ok. Let me pull them up." She quickly opened a folder on her laptop and opened the first image. "This one came from Jimmy, it appears to be an angry carrot."

Malcolm tilted his head as he looked at her screen. He saw what appeared to be a hand drawn doodle that was scanned in and coloured in some cheap photo editing software. "That does appear to be an angry carrot ... What does it say in the speech balloon?"

"Use Dataffair or get hacked. FA-Q!" Andrea was puzzled by the last bit until she had read it out loud. "Oh my. It says F-A-Q, not f..., well, not what it sounded like."

"Yeah, sounds right for Jimmy. OK, even as a temporary logo I don't think an angry carrot works. What else do we have?"

Andrea clicked on the next image and opened it. It was just text in a bold font that said "NO LOGO". "That one is from Matt ..." she said.

Malcolm looked at it for a second before shaking his head. "Nah, I'm sure we could have some weird marketing around what a bold choice we made, but ... nah, we need a logo. Next!"

Andrea brought up the next image displaying a white 'D' in a blue square with rounded corners. "Well at least this one looks like a logo. It's from Sachet."

"Hmm, it's pretty generic. Isn't the Facebook logo like that?" Malcolm pushed up on his glasses. "But they did lowercase right? I don't think I'd like a little D as much."

Andrea giggled, "Well no, who would right? It is pretty close to the Facebook logo, but it makes sense though, blue is a 'secure' colour, but we'd want to change it to our orange. And 'D' for Dataffair. I mean it's the best we've seen so far, even if it is simple."

"Very clean, appropriate and safe, exactly what I'd expect from Sachet. Alright let's see some more ..."

"Raj submitted this one ... I have no idea what it is. Dots with a cross in the middle maybe?" she pondered.

"It's a magic quadrant." sighed Malcolm. "Definitely Raj's work. It compares other companies to ours. See he's labelled the four areas made by the cross and put each company in one of those areas."

"Oh, I get it. That's weird. And he put us in the middle ..." she puzzled, "So we're a bit of everything?"

"I guess so. It's certainly not the best logo in the world. What else do we have?"

"There is only one more." replied Andrea, opening the last image. It was a silhouette of a woman with her finger to her lips inside a circle. Below the circle was "Dataffair: Don't get breached, have an affair." Andrea twisted her face, "I think I've seen this one before."

Malcolm leaned in closer to the screen. "You must've seen it when you printed them out for me. It's interesting." He cocked his head to the side, "I'm not sure about the slogan ..."

"Oh my God." exclaimed Andrea, "It's the Ashley Madison logo. Who submitted this?" She went back to the folder.

"Who's Ashley Madison?" asked Malcolm.

"It's that website where you go if you want to have an affair on your spouse. Their slogan is 'Life is short. Have an affair.'"

"Oh!" cried Malcolm. "OK, well we don't want that one. Was that Nasser?"

"Yes." sighed Andrea. "He must've just copied it off the web."

"And that's it? Those are the only options we received?"

"Well, if you remember, I wasn't allowed to enter ..."

"Oh yeah." muttered Malcolm, pushing his glasses up again. "Ok, well I like the D. I say we go with the D."

Andrea giggled. "This is why we need an HR department."

Malcolm turned to look at her, "What? You don't like the D?"

"Seriously," Andrea laughed, "You can't say that."

"Can't say what?" Malcolm stood up straight beside her. "I can't ask if you like it?"

"You can ask if I like the logo. Just not the D."

Malcolm's face contorted as he tried to sort out what was going on. "I'm not sure what we're talking about anymore. Are we still talking about the logo?"

"You really never get on social media do you?"

"No. I don't have time for that, what has that got to do with it, did someone already use a D? Discord, is that a social medium? If they have a big D then we'll just have a small d." he reasoned.

Andrea was laughing and just waved her hands in front of her.

"OK!" Malcolm had enough of whatever was going on. "I like the D. I say we're going with the D. If you don't like the D or someone else used the D before us that's fine. We'll change it later. Put the D in and we can take it out after."

Andrea's face was turning red and she was bent over her laptop laughing hysterically.

"You know what," said Malcolm calmly, "why don't you work from home tomorrow. I think you need a break." Malcolm shook his head and walked back to his own desk.

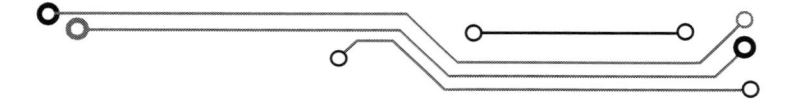

Malcolm Joffrey was the co-founder of Dataffair. Along with Gillian Cliff he had started the cybersecurity company in Waterloo, Ontario about two years ago. His team was reviewing the final draft of the Dataffair website before its launch.

Malcolm was scanning each page of the site systematically. He pushed up on the bridge of his steel rim glasses. It was a habit he had when deep in thought or worrying and it was causing a crease across his nose from how often he did it. He had a checklist open of "Common Mistakes in Website Design" in a tab of his browser. Another tab had a spreadsheet he was using to paste in the address of each page he reviewed. There were so many tabs open, the icon for each barely showed along the top of his browser.

Malcolm was six foot two, which his mom always said was

tall, but these days that seemed to feel average. Six foot four had become the new tall. He had to hunch over a bit to see his laptop sitting on the picnic table in front of him. He wore a checkered button up shirt, the same as every other day, and khaki shorts which he would switch to jeans when the weather turned. He wore the shirt untucked since he felt it made him appear hip and open to conversation. In reality he had to untuck it every morning while looking in the mirror, realizing he had already tucked it in out of habit.

He had a thick silver chain for the same reason and always made sure to leave his shirt unbuttoned enough that you could see the chain but it didn't fall out when he bent over. His hair was thin, but not thinning, it always fell back into the exact same position no matter what he did. His college friends had always been jealous as he just shook his head after swimming and his hair flopped back into place, as though he had just brushed it. Malcolm appreciated it, especially in toque season, when sweat and static would cause others to have hair going in every direction like a bird had made a nest in it, then given up on the nest and attempted to burn it, but Malcolm's hair was perfect.

Most of the Dataffair team was gathered around the picnic tables in the largest room of the office that served as lunch room, boardroom and only real meeting space. It wasn't like this because of any trendy startup appearances, it was just all they could afford. They had found a space with a reception area, two open rooms and a single office, and couldn't put any money into improvements.

The two picnic tables had been dragged there by some of the staff and one still had a chain around the leg, the table, not the staff member. Malcolm never bothered to ask where they got them. Since they were already carved and covered in graffiti the team used them to write notes, play Sudoku or doodle on. "Modern Edgy Convenience", Gillian had declared their decorating style.

They had been able to take over a lease from a failed startup and Malcolm was thrilled to have it. They had just moved right in without even bothering to clean up. The building itself was a typical, one-storey, concrete strip mall in an industrial park, but it was close to the expressway and public transit and the price was right. There was a custom dog toy manufacturer on one side and a business that rented out enormous inflatable animals on the other. Dataffair could rent the 20 foot gorilla for 50% off if they ever needed it.

You could still see where the previous company had hung their motivational posters, and the outline of their logo where the paint had faded on the reception area wall. Malcolm decided that the posters hadn't helped the last company and there was no point replacing them. The faded logo looked like a giant 'F' and Malcolm felt it would be disrespectful to paint over it.

Most of the team were working diligently to review every word and page of the website. Some discussion was taking place about the wording on the biographies page. Unfortunately, Andrea Miller, the marketing and social media manager Malcolm was talking to yesterday, had used the word "preeminent" when describing Raj, one of the developers. "Preeminent Computer Scientist, Rajesh Khatri, Ph.D, P.Eng, M.Eng". In an enterprise company, any issue with the wording could have been brought up with the Human Resources team, but when dealing with the type of individuals that fit a startup, things like this can become the entire afternoon. Everyone needed to get their two cents in, followed by three cents more, on whether they think the wording is right, the title is correct and most important, whether any of them should have a similar superfluous adjective.

Malcolm liked his own biography title: "Co-Founder Malcolm Joffrey, BSc., MBA." It allowed him to cross one more achievement off his bucket list. His next company, he would be sole founder and then who knows, great philanthropist or maybe corporate giant.

Both the co-founders were happy with the team they had been able to lure in. They had all been together for three months, some for more than a year, without anyone leaving for greener pastures (or more money, or stability, or other perks, or any perks really). They worked well together and dealt with their problems as a team, mostly. No one ever felt like they were on their own, they were almost a family now.

When they had dreamed up the company Dataffair, one of their goals was to start with a small, intelligent, creative team and then keep them together. Being in a startup environment with the same fifteen people for three months is an accomplishment and either creates a very tight, close knit team, or a frantic, frenzied, group of fanatics that collapse the whole business before you even begin. Malcolm at the time hadn't thought about conflicting personalities or whether the team "fit" together, he was worried about degrees, job pedigree, and talent. Gillian was the one who made sure they hired people that could deal with each other and get along. They managed to round out the team with co-operative students from the University that cycled in every three months.

"'If Raj is pre' eminent," Jimmy was saying, "then I need to be full out eminent." James "Jimmy" Bates was the build and tools developer at Dataffair. His job was to write software to keep the other developers working at peak efficiency. Without his tools Dataffair wouldn't be in the position they were, ready for website launch and soon, hopefully, the first customer. Jimmy wasn't big on "Production Development", he believed you coded till it was done and then you stopped. No tests, no refactoring, just do it right the first time. This is why he liked to stay in the tools department; the idea of having to add comments to everything he did, write tests, and optimize for different customers' needs made him lose interest in the whole job. If there wasn't a position like this for Jimmy, everyone was pretty sure he'd be a hacker. Jimmy wore nothing but hoodies and jeans (and the usual essentials). If it was 40 degrees Celsius outside, Jimmy was still in a hoodie and jeans. Every hoodie he owned had a different corporate logo on it and he had never paid for any of them.

"I already am fully eminent," said Raj. "Jimmy's right, can we change it to say "Fully Eminent Computer Scientist."" Rajesh had completed over 14 years of post-secondary education. He was lucky to have a job at all really, but managed to get some co-operative terms where he gained some real world experience that helped him acquire a position ... at a startup. His explanation of his long tenure at school was that he had a hard time deciding where to specialize, but his co-workers figured he just enjoyed the academic lifestyle. His jet black hair was always perfectly coiffed. At any point in time you could believe that he had just come from the barber. His silver glasses had thin rims that sparkled in the right light. He had an average build, not muscular, but there was no excess weight on him either. He was always dressed immaculately, no one ever saw Raj in a hoodie, or jeans. He was clean shaven and there was an air about him that exuded confidence and intelligence.

"Eminent ... What does that even mean? If you are eminent now, when were you pre-eminent?" questioned Sachet. As the only quality assurance team member, Sachet pretty much questioned absolutely everything. He believed that by doing so he was justifying his position at the company. Question authority and trust, but verify. Some startups didn't have a Quality Assurance team anymore, relying on the software developers to check their own work. There's a saying in the industry; You can't test quality in, you have to build it in. Malcolm and Gillian had both worked at companies like that and found it was always best to have someone picky as the gatekeeper and second set of eyes. It was a balance between accountability and getting things done. "Oh and do you get to be post-eminent? I want mine to say *Posteminent Quality Assurance Technical Authority*."

Sachet went into Quality Assurance right out of University, he had no desire to do anything else. His hair was short and parted on the side, he dressed like he had an inspection every day, his pant leg crease could cut you, and the rest of the team wondered if he ironed his socks. His dream was for Dataffair to grow and he would manage a large QA team across multiple continents.

"Ummm, eminent means respected within your position and preeminent is better than eminent guys." muttered Nasser Kennedy, another software developer. Rumour had it, he had grown up in an affluent family in India, no one really knew his family history. He had attended the University of Waterloo and been an early employee of Research In Motion before they were Blackberry. He lived in a 1980's backsplit on a beautiful court in the east end of Waterloo. It was a mystery how well off he made out at Research In Motion, they assumed because he was still working, it wasn't that great.

"Guys ... seriously. Look at the website." sighed Malcom. "Make sure you are documenting what browser and version you are using. Watch for spelling mistakes or any weird layout issues. Oh yeah, and Nasser is right, preeminent is better than eminent, it's like premier. Now get some work done!"

Less than a minute passed of silence.

Jimmy started it. "Ok, remember the prequels to Star Wars? They sucked hard. So it makes sense that 'quels' are better than prequels and therefore eminent is better than preeminent."

"Those weren't prequels, Jimmy," said Sachet. "The original Star Wars were in the middle starting at 4, so the new ones were just the beginning."

"Beginning of the end for me." muttered Jimmy.

"There's no such thing as a 'quel' even, that doesn't make sense." replied Sachet.

"If there's sequels and prequels, there must be quels. There must." said Jimmy.

"Just got to Mike's blob," Raj broke in, "are we seriously saying that he has over 40 years experience, doesn't that make him sound old?"

"He does have over 40 years experience. He said he didn't care if we even put his profile in since he plans to retire soon." replied Malcolm.

"Ha! But he won't. Where is Mike?" asked Sachet.

"He's in his office, working on the compression algorithm for our log data." answered Jimmy.

Mike Ziraldo was the only one in the company with an office. The rest, including the founders, worked in the second open area where they had set up makeshift desks using saw horses and old 1970's flat panel doors. Mike could do anything with digital data compression, zip it, flip it, mix it, stuff 100 lbs of data into a 1 lb blob. He had already worked at 3 companies that had gone public leaving him a multi-millionaire, yet for some reason he just wouldn't retire. He had over 100 classic arcade machines in his home and supposedly a barn full of more that he plans to fix "once he retires".

Mike was old school computer nerd; he had worked on one of the first PDP-11 computers in the 70's. Rumour had it that he proved the Collatz conjecture on that machine and just didn't bother to let anyone know. He wore a pocket protector with actual pens in it and wrote things down on paper ... in a log book. Mike worked his own schedule, he arrived most days around 10:00 a.m., played tri-peaks solitaire until noon then went for lunch. He napped between 1:00 and 3:00 and did amazing things from 3:00 until 4:30 when he left.

It was nearing 4:30 now. Malcolm pushed his hair back with both hands, then pushed his glasses against his nose again. "Alright guys, I'll look at this tonight when I get home. Sachet, what build did we approve of the new rules engine?"

Dataffair was a cybersecurity company. The plan was for customers to run the Dataffair software and it would be able to find anomalies in the logs of their other software to alert them of a hacking attempt or data exfiltration. The software developers at Dataffair wrote rules that their artificial intelligence server could use to identify these threats. Of course, no customers were running these rules right now, because Dataffair didn't have any customers. Malcolm and Gillian had both agreed that they would have a product first, and then build a customer base. They'd seen others attempt to start selling before their product was ready and usually it led to products that matched the initial customer, instead of finding customers that matched your product.

"0.5.1034 is the last beta build" replied Sachet, "Total green lights all the way, we can ship it anytime."

"Jimmy, did you get the deployment service actually working this time, or do we still need to do this in stages?" asked Malcom.

"All set. We can deploy directly from the tested build to groups of customers or the whole shebang at once. In fact, we could deploy customer by customer with a timer in between that ..."

"Awesome. Thanks Jimmy." Malcolm cut him off and looked at his watch. 4:25 p.m. Gillian should be arriving any time. She liked to enjoy the day and work in the evening, sometimes all through the night until Malcolm showed up again in the morning. "Once Gillian is here, check with her and if she's good with it I say we ship it. Website goes live in the morning assuming I don't find anything tonight and we're ready to find customer zero."

"Oh man," whined Nasser, "but this job is so easy with no customers."

"Yeah for you guys." smiled Malcolm.

"Ok, I'm going back to my desk, these picnic tables need to learn about ergonomics." said Raj and picked up his laptop as he eased out of the bench.

Cheryl LaFontaine walked in from the reception area in a bee line for the fridge. Cheryl handled the financials, human resources, event planning (with Andrea's help) and managed the office. If there was anything the team needed, Cheryl was the person to get it. "Hey all, I'm doing groceries tomorrow morning on the way in, if you want something it better be on this list." The fridge had a magnetic whiteboard attached to it where the team could pick what snacks and beverages they wanted to be magically in the fridge the next week.

"Oh man, did anyone put meat sticks on there?" asked Jimmy.

"Yes, pepperettes are listed here 3 times, and 'meat sticks' twice." answered Cheryl, taking a picture of the list with her phone.

"Sweeeeeeet." hummed Jimmy. He flung himself out of the table, strolled over and grabbed a hard cider from the fridge. "It's beer o'clock, people! I'm heading back to my desk." He picked up his laptop with one hand and headed to the open area. "Oh yeah, and I'd like my bio to say 'Prominent Software Toolsmith'" he yelled back as he left to many groans and curses.

"Prominent Tool!" Nasser yelled back.

"Malcolm, do you want anything special for the website launch tomorrow?" asked Cheryl.

"I guess we should have a cake. Oh and pies for the weird people that prefer pie over the purest form of sweetness that is cake." chirped Malcolm.

"Pie is greater than cake and everyone knows it." said Nasser. "Pie comes in so many forms! It can be sweet or savoury, just the number of different consistencies that can still be pie is amazing."

"Your pie affliction is well known Nasser, I don't want to get into why cake is better right now. The important part is we can get writing on the cake, nobody writes on pie." Malcolm paused. "I think it should say 'Congratulations Dataffair on Initial Launch'".

"People could write on pie." Nasser whined as he looked back at his screen.

Matt Reynolds who had been studying his laptop with intensity looked up. Matt was the system architect for the company, all software design decisions went through him. He had a mop of rusty hair with a shaggy beard that he rarely trimmed. He wore camo cargo shorts every day. The shorts had different colours in them, but they were all camouflage based. Snow camo, desert camo, jungle camo, grasslands camo, he had them all. Matt was always in a geek culture T-shirt, and no one had ever seen him wear the same shirt twice. It was becoming a bit of a contest with the group to catch him in a shirt he'd already worn. Today's shirt said "Life's a Breach" with a silhouette of a hacker at a laptop. "Did you just say 'Day-ta-fair'? I don't think I've ever heard the company name pronounced before."

"Yeah, Dataffair." said Malcolm.

"I've been pronouncing it Dah-ta-fair in my head." said Matt.

"Ha!" laughed Nasser, "Like 'What affair? Dat Affair!'"

"No it's Dataffair." said Malcolm, "Like the way you are supposed to pronounce data."

"Oh, hey, I solved the day-ta versus dah-ta problem at my last job while I was bored." Sachet chimed in. "It's simple really, if it's all in capitals it's DATA and if it's in lower case it's data."

"Really?" questioned Matt. "It's been that simple all along." he remarked sarcastically, pushing himself up from the table. "Fine, I'll check with Mike. Mike was there when they came up with the word."

Matt walked over to the single office. Mike was packing up his log book into his attaché case. "Hey Mike," Matt said as he chose a whiteboard marker from the tray attached to the wall. "What does this say?" Matt stroked out DATA in large block letters on the whiteboard.

"DATA." said Mike.

"Mmm hmm, and what does this say?" Matt wrote 'data' below the previous line.

"Data." answered Mike.

"Holy crap, he's right." muttered a stunned Matt. "SACHET! You were right, Mike confirmed it. That blows me away."

"I told you!" came a yelled response.

Mike gave a half hearted smile, not really knowing what was going on and picked up his case. "C'ya tomorrow everyone." He walked across the open area and out the back door to his car.

Matt spoke to the room in general, "I gotta go talk to Raj, I think he's the only other one that doesn't have a hackathon team for next week. See if we can get together and come up with something brilliant." This was to be the Dataffairs second annual hackathon. It was a time for them to create whatever they wanted instead of following the roadmap of the company. They spent three pretty much sleepless days designing, building and presenting their idea of how to make the company better.

"Oh yeah, hackathon," said Malcolm. "Three days where I get no real work out of you guys." he smiled. Last year's projects were actually really good. One of them had become part of their main product.

At this point Gillian walked into the main area. She was tall, with dark hair dyed purple at the ends. She had round glasses with blue lenses and big hoop earrings. She was wearing bell-bottom jeans with sandals and a t-shirt with a drawing of a kitten giving the finger. "Hey everybody!"

"Gillian, we're called Dataffair right?" said Malcolm.

"Exactly, why?"

"Matt's been saying DATAffair in his head this whole time."

"I say we fire him immediately." she joked.

"Done. We're just deciding what to put on the cake for tomorrow."

"Oh, cake! Awesome. Let's put 'Way to go Team Awesome. Blow shit up!'" gesturing with her arms an explosion of epic proportions and making detonation noises that slowly trailed off as she looked at Malcolm's face.

"Oh yeah, that'll be great in the photo gallery when they build the museum about us."

Gillian laughed. "Whatever you put is fine. I'm just glad we got here. Launch day! Speaking of which, we have that sales VP interview tomorrow."

"Ok, I'm going with the congratulations line." Cheryl spoke up as she headed back out towards reception. "See you guys tomorrow. It's going to be great."

"Bye Cheryl!" The group sang in unison as some waved.

"You said you've worked with this sales guy before, right?" questioned Malcolm, turning back to Gilllian. Gillian and Malcolm had both been with other startups before. Malcolm had been Employee 7 and Employee 19 at two startups that went public, but had always dreamed of being a founder. Gillian had started over 10 companies, none of which ever became wildly successful. Some flopped completely and others were bought up before they got off the ground. She had invested most of her money from the sales into the next startup each time. The two had met at a founders networking breakfast. Malcolm was Employee 6, with a C-title at a startup then, which is how they came up with the portmanteau of Data and Affair since they were registering this company before he had officially left the last company.

Malcolm was keen on learning how Gillian could be so laid back about running a company, his own style was too close to micro management and he knew it. You could manage every detail of a startup but as it grew to enterprise level you had to know how to let go. He'd love to stress less and enjoy the ride the way Gillian did. And what did he have to worry about, he had the penthouse condo downtown, set his parents up in Florida and could retire now without any worries. He just always wanted that "Founder" tag and the recognition that came with it. Dataffair was his chance to make a name for himself.

"Yeah I worked with him at FloraBona, my plant-share company, he managed sales for me." Gillian just enjoyed the thrill of starting from nothing and building. She didn't believe it mattered what you built as long as you were creating.

"And how did that go?" laughed Malcolm.

"Hey! Sales weren't the problem. We had florists and gardeners swapping plants all over the country, we just didn't think about FDA restrictions and how obsessed people can get over the pedigree of certain plants that we didn't expect to be travelling through our system."

Malcolm laughed again. "Well, the good news is, we should be able to avoid being pot dealers in this case."

"We weren't exactly pot dealers! We were just supporting the artisanal, hand grown, recreational drug enthusiasts by accident. Plus, it's legal in lots of places … now."

Nasser got up from the table. "I'll let you guys talk shop, I'm going to get some headphone time at my desk. I'm hoping to have the new user interface done by tomorrow. Which means you'll be able to run your tests first thing in the morning, Sachet."

"Yeah, I can do that." replied Sachet. "And I wanted to talk to you about the date picker anyway, I'll walk back to your desk with you. The big problem is the 32nd of January, 1984."

"Why would anyone be choosing 1984 as the year?" questioned Nasser as they were walking out.

"Then why is 1984 in the date picker? And still, why does it have a 32nd of January?"

"How do you even find this shit?" was the last thing Malcolm and Gillian heard.

Malcolm smiled and turned back to Gillian, "So this guy that we're interviewing wasn't involved in the drug scandal right?"

"Nooo no no." She drew out the last "no" to the point Malcolm got worried, "He was awesome. He grew the sales organization and you'll like him, he's all about the numbers."

"I hope so, we need to go from 0 to 1,000 really quick."

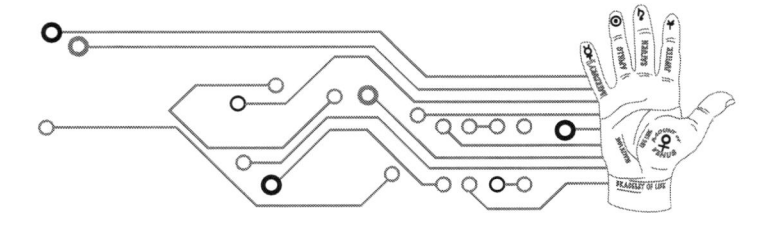

CHAPTER 0000 0001: ENTER NOLAN

Launch Day. Cheryl was in from the grocery shopping by 8:00 a.m. In her three trips to the car she brought in the weekly supply of snacks as well as the box containing the huge slab cake. She placed the box on one of the picnic tables. Flipping the lid back she stared into the box with a skeptical expression on her face. Her red hair was in a bob cut that swirled around her face as she shook her head.

"Congratulations Data Fair on Initial Lunch" was written in flowing blue script across white icing. There had been only one cake available at this time of day and Cheryl had bought it. There were flowers in the corners and reminded her more of a funeral than a corporate event.

"Maybe they won't notice …" she muttered to herself, wiping her hands on her skirt. She considered attempting to smudge the typos with her finger, but decided against it. A poorly spelled cake was better than one that someone had run their fingers through, she decided. She closed the box. If she was able to cut it up and serve it before anyone actually saw it all together, they'd never be able to piece it back together.

She went back to the car for the various flavours of pies. After storing them away she began to turn on all the lights. She could see Jimmy coming in from his car. She was pretty sure he was still wearing the same clothes as yesterday. His backpack with laptop in it was over one shoulder and he was carrying a large paper cup with "Jimmy B" written on it.

"LAUNCH DAY!!" he bellowed as he came into the office. "Hey Cheryl, meat sticks in the fridge?"

"Yep. On sale too, so I stocked up for hackathon next week."

"SWEEET!!" he cheered.

"I don't know where you get your energy in the morning." she laughed.

"Caffeine! Coffee makes the world go round," he raised his cup in the air. He leaned into the fridge and grabbed two pepperettes before heading to the work area. "Gotta get to it Cheryl. It's going to be exciting today."

Nasser was the next to arrive. Coming into the reception he asked Cheryl, "Have you seen Sachet this morning?"

"Not yet." she replied.

"Ok, hopefully he won't be long, I worked until almost midnight last night to get that UI done." he walked towards the lunch room, "What kind of pies did you get? I've been craving a banana creme for some reason."

"Oh, no banana creme, but apple, strawberry-rhubarb, chocolate and a lemon meringue."

"Well it'll have to do." he smiled. "Alright, off to it, have a good day."

"You too."

The rest of the team slowly trickled in over the next hour. Malcolm was surprised that Gillian wasn't still there, but figured she must have actually wanted to sleep for the big day. "Did that sales guy's flight arrive last night?" he asked Cheryl.

"Yes, he actually called me last night to let me know he had landed and was settling in."

"Awesome. Looking forward to meeting him." Malcolm said. The candidate's name was Nolan Walker. He had flown in from Silicon Valley last night and was staying for a week. Partially for the interview, but apparently also to get together with some previous associates and have a few drinks. In enterprise software it was rare not to have a previous associate wherever you travelled.

"Is that the cake?" asked Malcolm, tiptoeing over to the table.

"Umm, yes." Cheryl slowly replied. "No peeking. I'm not sure how I'm going to present it yet."

"Not sure how you're going to present it?" Malcolm repeated as a question, "Like there's a possibility of fireworks and smoke machines?"

Cheryl giggled, "Not like that, I just mean I may pre-plate it to keep the line moving."

"Oh. Less exciting." Malcolm came back to her desk, "So the plan is to take him out for lunch and then have him here for the launch celebration, let him meet the team and see our culture."

"Sounds good. I'll make sure everything is set up." Malcolm knew she wasn't kidding. Cheryl made sure their office ran like a dream. He never had to worry about anything from missing payroll to running out of Post-It notes. Cheryl made sure everything went perfect.

"Awesome." Malcolm started to walk through the lunch area on his way to his desk. He wanted this interview to go well. It was always good to hire a vice president of sales first and let them build their own team. He just wanted the right vice president, someone who knew how to talk to people, could sell the product themselves at the beginning, but hired the right people to grow their team. It was also critical that the sales team and the research and development team got along. He'd been with a few companies where it became a feud between them and the company always lost when that happened.

He said his "Good mornings" to the staff and sat down at his desk. After connecting his computer to his monitors he pulled up his spreadsheet from last night. There were only a few minor problems he had found with the website and he was happy with it overall. He checked the company's private chat application to see if Andrea was online. She was, so he sent her the spreadsheet file with a smiley emoji writing "Just a few updates and we can pull down the Under Construction page."

Matt came into the office shortly after nine. "Good morning Cheryl." he said as he passed her desk. "You can put Raj and I down as a team for the hackathon, we're calling ourselves 'Psi Phi', we are going to use our higher sense perception and the golden ratio to create a mesmerizing display of computational insight that's going to blow away the competition." He sounded like he was giving her an elevator pitch.

"Ok good." said Cheryl, unenthused by the speech. She opened the hackathon spreadsheet on her computer. "I'll put you guys down to present last so we go out with a bang." she said sarcastically.

"Awesome. No idea what we're going to do yet, but it's going to be amazeballs, as the kids say." Matt skipped through the kitchen on his way to his desk. Malcolm was on his way back to the reception area and laughed at the antics as they passed. He had felt Matt was a good hire right from the beginning. Matt was a brilliant system designer and had tremendous insight not just into the code, but the costs and platforms and systems that made up a business. Aside from that he was fun, which Malcolm knew would draw in more good hires. It was a circle Malcolm had learned early on as you watched good people leave together and stay together.

"Gillian is still not here?" he asked Cheryl, leaning on her desk.

"Not yet." replied Cheryl with a sigh. "Do you want me to phone her? It is only 2 and half hours until she has to be here."

Malcolm grimaced. "No. That's fine." He tapped his fingers on her desk and Cheryl went back to her typing. "Unless," he said and Cheryl looked back at him, "Unless you think you should call her?"

"No, I think she'll be here, same as she's always here when needed." Cheryl rolled her eyes and continued her work.

"Ok." said Malcolm, and ended his desk drumming with a big solo that would have made Neal Peart embarrassed. "I'll go check how Andrea is doing on the website release." He looked at his phone for the time and checked if there were any messages. "Yeah, I'll go check on that." He slowly walked across the kitchen, his eyes never leaving his phone, even as he pushed his glasses back.

Sachet could be seen running down the sidewalk outside, his backpack flipping from side to side as he chugged towards the main entrance. He heaved the door open and rushed inside.

"My magnalarm didn't activate." he said to Cheryl as he rushed by. She had no idea what that meant, she didn't care what that meant.

"Nasser is looking for you." she called out to his back as he headed across the kitchen.

Sachet was doing a walking run as he entered the main area.

"No speed-walking in the office." Jimmy yelled from his own desk. "Someone's gotta do health and safety around here," he laughed.

Sachet went straight to his desk, flopped his backpack on his chair and started to pull out his laptop. Nasser could easily see him of course, one of the unfortunate parts of having a wide open space. Sachet grimaced as Nasser got up from his chair and began to walk over. He quickly connected his monitors, mouse and keyboard. It was easy because he had his cables all zip tied together in a row and labelled.

"I was hoping that we'd get that new interface tested first thing this morning." said Nasser as he approached.

"I know, I know." said Sachet, "My magnalarm didn't activate this morning. I'm way behind."

"What's a magnalarm?" asked Nasser.

Sachet sat down and was logging into his computer. He answered quickly, never looking up from his machine. "I built the ultimate alarm clock. The sound comes from the TV in the living room. I have to get up and enter the code on the TV into my phone to disable it. Once I do that, another alarm goes off in the kitchen in 5 minutes if I don't start the coffee maker by then. There's one more in the bathroom if it doesn't detect shower water running."

"That's insane, you know that right?"

"Sure, sure, but I updated my network configuration last night and the alarm server couldn't talk to the TV. I never even thought about it. Now my entire schedule is messed up. I didn't even eat this morning."

"Wow."

"I didn't watch the news, I haven't had a coffee, seriously, just give me a minute to get myself together." said Sachet, still typing and not looking at Nasser.

"Sure, sure. Ping me when you're back to normal."

Nasser was walking back to his desk and noticed Gillian was just sitting down in her chair. He had never seen her in the office this early and remembered it was launch day. He strolled over to her desk. "Hey Gillian, good to see you at this hour of the day."

"Hey Nasser," she replied, spinning her chair to face him. "How's it going?" Gillian was excellent at talking to people. All of the staff felt like she was their best friend. Her body language always presented a calm, attentive and open attitude that just drew people in.

"Good, I have the new interface done, just waiting for Sachet to run his tests and we can push it live before customer zero". Programmers had a habit of starting to count at 0 instead of 1. It was all due to a guy named Martin Richards many years ago.

"You guys and your customer zero, you make it sound like customers are an infectious disease." she said and laughed.

"Hey, let's hope so! Once we get one, it'll spread." he laughed as well.

"Nice." she commented with a little smile that made her eyes get large. "Let's be customertagious!" Nasser gave her the so-so sign for that one. "So, who's on your hackathon team?" She slyly changed the subject.

"It's Andrea, Daniel and I. We're going to build a new rule for detecting breached passwords on the dark web. Should be alright, why are you looking for a team?"

"I haven't found one yet, I may just skip the crazy and watch the presentations at the end." said Gillian, picturing having a few days to actually work on their slide deck for investors instead of spending it plugging away on code.

"Well you should talk to Matt, I think he was looking for someone." said Nasser, trying to be helpful.

"Thanks, I'll do that." she said, looking past him as she noticed Malcolm standing directly behind him. "Looks like I'm needed."

she said pointing around Nasser's side. "Talk to you later."

"Oh hey Matt, the new interface is going to be tested shortly, I'll keep you posted." said Nasser turning around. He walked past him as he headed back to his own desk and said over his shoulder, "Sachet's magnalarm couldn't talk to his television, so you know how that is."

"Oh sure, that's understandable" said Malcolm and turned to Gillian, "What's a magnalarm?"

"I have no idea." she said.

Gillian drove them to the interview. They were meeting with Nolan at The Code and Clam, a local seafood pub that took advantage of the amount of technology companies in Waterloo. Malcolm wasn't a huge fan of having someone else drive, he didn't like giving up control, but he wanted to peruse Nolan's resume again on the way over, so he didn't complain.

Nolan was there before them. He stood as they approached the table. Dressed in a gray blazer over a black turtleneck with dark grey pants. Malcolm wondered if his monochromatic look was so that nothing distracted from his gleaming teeth, trendy half-rim glasses and shiny hair. Were people still greasing their hair? Malcolm wondered. Nolan was in good shape, he was obviously muscular and standing about 6'3" he filled out his clothes with bulges everywhere Malcolm wished he had bulges, he always felt like he was destined to be the skinny guitar player and never the muscled drummer. Nolan was clean shaven with just the right amount of sideburns. Not 70's style and not trimmed to the ear, Malcolm found himself questioning his own shaving choices that morning just looking at them.

"Gillian! It's so good to see you again." said Nolan enthusiastically. He wrapped her in a big hug before she could get a word out. "And you must be Malcolm," he continued, breaking the hug in one fluid motion and pushing his hand out towards Malcolm. His handshake was a "sales" handshake. Malcolm wondered if they practiced that sort of thing, firm enough that you felt like your hand was truly being held, but gentle enough you felt like you could stop the shake at any time. "It's great to meet you. Gillian has said great things about you, looking forward to getting to know you and hearing all about Dataffair."

Gillian was expecting to do the introductions, but saw that she wasn't going to get a word in and put her purse over the back of her chair as she sat down.

"It's great to meet you, Nolan. Gillian has also been talking about you. I can't wait to hear what you can do for us if we decide to move forward."

The lunch started with small talk of the weather variations when you fly over 4,000 km across North America, and the conditions at the hotel where Dataffair had put Nolan up. Mostly he discussed the pillow at the hotel. He seemed obsessed with it and it's head cradling perfection. Malcolm began to worry that Nolan's skills would be better used in the bedding industry rather than technology. Once their food arrived, Nolan finally asked a relevant question.

"I'm interested in the hardware aspects. Will you be leasing them your servers, direct sales, or supplying them as part of the service fee?" he asked.

"Good question. We're including the hardware in the fee. That allows us to send upgraded hardware when required. We don't want customers turning down necessary updates to the device just because they don't want to pay for a new one." replied Malcolm.

"In a perfect world we wouldn't have a device at all." interjected Gillian. "We'd like to eventually run a central AI server in the cloud and have the customers send data directly to our own cloud services."

"Through some type of encrypted virtual private network?" asked Nolan.

"Exactly." replied Gilian.

Malcolm was starting to come on board, maybe Nolan knew more than the proper pillow for a side sleeper. "But," he jumped in, "that's not for a few more years. Initially every client will need our device attached directly to their network. We've put in a purchase order with our supplier for 1,000 to start."

"And will they provision them with your software?" asked Nolan.

"Yes and no. They want to provision all 1,000 at once, so they will be ready, but they'll be running whatever software version we have available when they ship the first one."

"Having a device in the customers location, you should be charging an onboarding fee, you know someone is going to have to get out there and help them out, or you're going to get support calls for sure. Need a way to recoup some of those costs." said Nolan like he was their business mentor. Malcolm found himself being lured in.

"Malcolm was asking me earlier about how you grow your sales team." said Gillian, "Perhaps you can fill him in on that."

"Does anybody call you Malc?" asked Nolan.

"Definitely not." replied Malcolm.

"Gotcha." Nolan said with a smile and leaned over the table on his elbows. "Malcolm, I've basically created the sales mafia." He leaned even closer and Malcolm was becoming uncomfortable with the amount of eye contact. "You see, I realized I'm not in the business of selling stuff, I'm in the business of selling."

Malcolm wasn't sure what that meant. "Selling what?" he asked.

"Just selling. It's like you programmer guys, you don't just program one thing, right? No. You're a computer programmer so you program anything you want. I'm a sales guy, I need to sell. So I've got a team together across the globe of other dedicated sales people. We don't work for the companies we're selling for, we work as a team to sell. Sales is our product, get it? Let's face it, when sales drop for some company, it's not the sales team's fault. It's that the market has changed, or the product has lagged behind." He waved his hand absently as though shooing away a fly. "A true sales person can't work for one company, they have to work for all companies. Wherever there are sales to be made, that's where you find the sales mafia." his eyes drifted to the ceiling and Malcolm believed he was trying to picture who would play him in the movie of his life.

"I'm still not understanding. Are you saying you don't want to work for Dataffair, but you'll sell our service on the side?" Malcolm questioned, he pushed his glasses back on his nose and looked at Gillian, mostly just to break Nolan's eye contact. Did this guy ever blink?

"Oh no, I think Dataffair is where I want to be. The product sounds great, the margins look good, and cybersecurity has massive growth potential. This is what the sales mafia is all about. We find services and products exactly like yours, ones that are headed to the moon, and then we all get together and sell the shit out of them. One hundred percent on board, banking dollars, and building empires. But every empire falls eventually. At some point something else that needs selling more comes along, then we all shift to that and leave the fools that aren't in our little family holding the bag. When

I bring this up to the group they are going to be all over it. They'll drop whatever else they are doing, because again, they are in sales and this product has sales written all over it. They aren't in video projectors or compilers or whatever it is they happen to be selling right now, you get it?"

Malcolm wasn't sure he was hearing this right. This was becoming a bizarre interview on sales psychology. He needed to think. "What do you think? Gillian" he asked to give himself a mental break.

"Oh yeah, this is how Nolan built our sales team at FloraBona so fast." she said.

"And the mafia was just little then. Wait till you see who we've got now. See, we train the sales associates below us, then bring them into the fold. We don't train them however the corporate process says, we train them to be the best in sales. They're like sales ninjas. Top secret sales teams spread across the globe that can sell anything." Nolan was getting more animated as he talked. Malcolm wondered if he was on something.

"But didn't they all wind up being drug dealers?" asked Malcolm.

"That's part of what gave me the mafia idea!" Nolan laughed. "Look, I'm telling you, I'll build your sales scripts over the next month and we'll start putting your devices in customer locations within the month. And once it starts, we will absolutely crush this industry. That gives us an October start and I'm thinking of a million in sales by the end of the year. Stop that cash burn startups all have and begin that climb to profitability."

"Well that part definitely sounds good," said Malcolm. He tried to read what Gillian was thinking from her face, but she was smiling and rolling her seafood linguine onto a fork.

"Nolan is the best." She said, "If he believes in the product, he can sell it. I mean this is the guy who sold our FloraBona contract to HGTV for all their landscaping shows."

Malcolm was twisting his lips into a side pucker and staring at Nolan as he was cracking crab legs against the side of the table. You can always let people go, he was thinking. And they had no one else to lead their sales team right now. He was racking his brain for anyone that he could poach from somewhere, but really at the moment, he was ready to just let Gillian have this one. Worse came to worst he could let him go and Gillian would owe him one.

"Did you want to come tour the office and meet the team?" he asked.

"That sounds excellent!" said Nolan, half a crab leg in each hand.

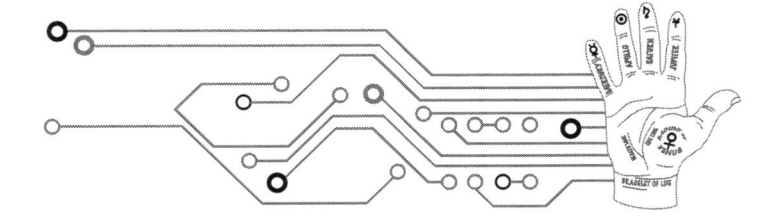

CHAPTER 0000 0010: LUNCH DAY

Nolan stuffed himself into the back of Gillian's Mazda 3 and they drove back to the office. Malcolm found his fish tacos were sitting pretty heavy during the ride. He hoped the office was looking professional for their guest and the team would be in good spirits. Nolan commented that he was surprised that Gillian drove manual transmission and Malcolm rolled his eyes. "I'm not saying it's just women that don't drive stick." Nolan tried to explain, "no one drives manual anymore. Unless it's a sports car." It was becoming apparent to Malcolm that although Nolan could apparently sell anything, he was not exactly up to date on the world.

Gillian took it in stride, shifting into fourth as she entered the expressway. "Well, this is a Mazda-rati." Nolan laughed. "I've always driven manual," she commented, "I grew up on a farm, so learned early on tractors and dirt bikes." Malcolm looked over at her, he hadn't known that. He realized he actually didn't know anything about her history. He knew she attended the University of Waterloo and had majored in nanotechnology, he could name all of the businesses she had started and even list most of their financial information. He had no idea where she was born.

"I didn't know you grew up on a farm," he remarked. "What did you farm?"

"It was a dairy farm. Milking over 150 head." she replied. "My brother still runs it, I get down there once in a while."

"I would never have made it as a farmer." remarked Nolan. "The only kind of farm I've dealt with is pharmacology if you know what I mean." Nolan laughed at his own joke. Malcolm rolled his eyes in the front seat and went back to looking out the window. The office was in an industrial complex right off the expressway, he could see it now. Someday they would need a sign on the building that you could see from here. It would really help get the business some notoriety. Of course, if they grew fast enough, they'd need a new building shortly after that.

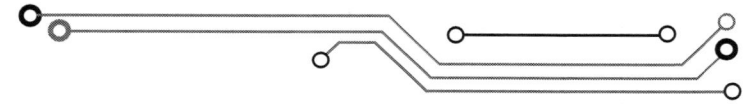

As Nolan got out of the car he was already commenting. "I love it. Great location." Malcolm thought Nolan strolled into the building like he owned the place. He flung open the front door so fast Malcolm thought it would come off its hinges. He approached the inner door with one step and a huge smile. "This place is awesome," he was saying as Malcolm grabbed the door behind him before it shut Gillian and him out.

Malcolm could see Cheryl rising from her desk and coming around to greet Nolan. Nolan didn't really need introductions, stretching his hand out to Cheryl before she could even get to him. "Nolan Walker, looking at the sales VP position. How are you today?"

Cheryl caught his hand and gave him a quick shake. "I'm doing well, thanks for asking. I'm Cheryl, the office manager. I arranged your flight and hotel."

"Cheryl! Yes, we talked on the phone last night. So great to put a face to the voice. Hotel is excellent. The pillows there are something else, if you can get me the product name on those I'd appreciate it." with that he wrapped Cheryl in a bear hug. "I'm a hugger." he said. Malcolm was watching Cheryl look like a penguin with her arms stuck out under Nolan's immense hug. She was looking straight at him with her eyebrows raised in a state of shock.

"I can see that." she said. "Avoid Mike. Mike's not a hugger."

"Great advice, thanks!" said Nolan and strode into the kitchen area without waiting for the others.

"Wow, he's something," said Cheryl. Malcolm was still watching Nolan's back disappear and pushed up his glasses.

Gillian smiled and said "He's a hugger." Then she laughed. Cheryl laughed as well, but Malcolm just shook his head.

"Hopefully he can fit into our culture if we bring him on board." Right now Malcolm was worried that Nolan would become the culture.

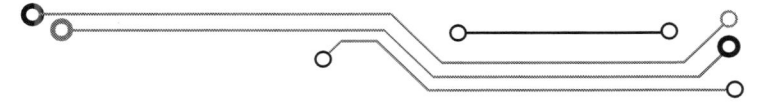

The whole team was there for the big launch lunch. Malcolm stood at the end of the picnic tables with Gillian and Cheryl and surveyed the team. They were all sitting on the picnic tables eating the cake of lies as it had come to be known. Nasser of course was eating pie. If Malcolm hadn't known better he would have said Nolan had been lifelong friends with all of them. Even now, Mike was talking to him about arcade machines and Mike didn't really talk to anyone.

Cheryl started "I'm glad everyone could make it in today. We have the whole team here to celebrate the launch of our website as well as the launch of our first service, the Dataffair Log Driver. I apologize for the 'Cake of Lies' as you all are calling it, it was a bit rushed. We have one guest with us today, Nolan Walker who is applying for the position of VP of sales, I hope you all offer him a warm welcome. A reminder that the forks are made of recycled paper as well as the plates and they can all go in the compost. Now Malcolm and Gillian would like to say a few words."

Everyone clapped loudly, and the group of sixteen sounded like a full auditorium to Malcolm. Nolan let out a whoop, and Jimmy followed with a whistle.

"Thank you, thank you!" said Gillian, stepping forward as Cheryl went to the fridge to grab a vodka soda. "Everyone here deserves the praise for getting us to today. There is no one that hasn't been a key component part of the process. With a team this size, we all have to work together. We don't point fingers of blame and we all share the praise. The Log Driver service is going to help our customers find indicators of compromise faster, and will keep their data safe from hackers. We are providing a service that makes a difference, you can all be proud of that. Congratulations to everyone! Cheers!" She raised her own can of beer and everyone joined in with a round of hollers and chants.

Malcolm stepped forward still clapping. "Thanks Gillian, that was a great reminder that we are all here for the same purpose." Everyone settled into their seats a little deeper. Malcolm was known for being long-winded and dry. He noticed this change and was determined to keep his speech lighter.

"We are currently sitting on a cash-burn of just over one hundred thousand dollars a month." he started. "With our initial investment money, this will keep us afloat for another 6 months." He could see the faces of the team start to straighten. At least they were getting the idea. "Now is when we need to start bringing on customers and revenue and I can safely say with what I've seen from this team, that's not going to be a problem."

"I know you all work hard, and you're going to have to keep working just as hard to get this rocket we've fired out of orbit and to the moon. Your efforts so far have been tremendous and I'm so proud of the team we have here at Dataffair. I can't wait to be standing here in six months telling you that not only are we moving forward, but we're growing."

"Maybe we can get actual desks!" Jimmy shouted from his seat and everyone laughed.

"Maybe." Malcolm shrugged. "And maybe in a few years, we'll all get Lamborghinis!" he shouted and everyone started to holler again.

"On a serious note, congratulations to the entire team. When Gillian and I decided to create this company it wasn't a light decision. We knew we'd need the right talent and a team that stuck together. I believe we have found that team and this rocket isn't just going to the moon, we're going to sail right past it. Everyone here wants to be part of the next big thing and that's why we have the best team in the business. Cheers!"

Everyone started to clap and holler again. Nasser was banging the table "Here, here!" Even Mike was smiling.

Cheryl trotted to the front, "Before everyone goes back to 'work'," she put air quotes up around the word work. "I wanted to give a few announcements. Next Monday is Thanksgiving Day so don't forget to take the day off. I'm looking at you Raj." Raj had come into work on almost every holiday and wondered why everyone else didn't do the same.

"The rest of you all are slackers" he said pointing around the tables, he scrunched his eyebrows together to try and appear angry, but it wasn't working.

Cheryl continued "And that means our hackathon starts on Wednesday. I believe everyone has teams already and we will cater lunch on Wednesday and Thursday. I've booked dinner for Friday at the Code and Clam for the entire team. At dinner we will present the awards for best hackathon project based on the presentations Friday afternoon. Anyone have any questions?"

"What is the judging rubric?" asked Sachet half raising his hand before noticing that he had already asked.

Gillian stepped up, "Great question, we haven't actually decided on the final judges yet, but we will be judging on the melon rubric. Does it sound hollow? In our case, you don't want that, we want meaningful projects. Does it look good? Presentation counts, make your pitch with some gusto. Is it ripe? Projects that we can start using right away will be graded higher than those that need a lot more work to productize."

"Does it go splat if you drop it?" shouted Jimmy and everyone laughed.

"Alright everyone," Malcolm spoke up. "Can I get Andrea to go live with the website?" Malcolm directed attention with his hands to the first picnic table where Andrea opened her laptop screen and tapped at the keys to log in. She opened up a couple apps and the rest of the team either leaned in to look at her screen or began refreshing the site on their own laptops. Matt had his laptop projecting onto the big screen mounted on the wall that normally displayed metrics data. Everyone could only see "Coming Soon. Contact us for more information." displayed in white block letters on a blue background.

Suddenly the big display changed to a vibrant screen with

orange and yellow gradients across the background displaying a web of curved beams shooting around the globe. The menu was simple and obvious at the top right. The Dataffair logo took up the majority of the upper left with its stylized lowercase 'd' in an orange rounded square, with the caption "We know what's going on."

There was a slow clap started by Nolan and soon everyone was in on it. "Congratulations Dataffair" Nolan bellowed and then everyone let loose.

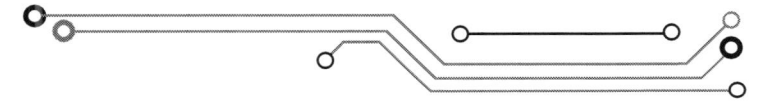

It was 7:00 p.m. and Raj, Matt and Jimmy were still sitting at the picnic tables and playing a card game someone had brought in. Jimmy was single and took the light rail transit to work. He had obviously been enjoying the open fridge all afternoon. Matt had a family, but didn't like to leave until either Malcolm or Gillian did. Raj seemed to just never go home, and when he did, it was to work remotely. Nolan had left to meet up with his contacts saying he'd probably stick around for the next week and enjoy Canadian Thanksgiving with his friends. Jimmy had responded with the mandatory "Up here we just call it Thanksgiving."

Malcolm and Gillian sat sideways at their desks side by side. He had a Scotch which was the only thing he drank. Gillian had a large glass of Pinot Grigio. She was twisting her wrist and watching the wine swirl around the edge of the glass. She believed Malcolm only drank Scotch so he could name what kind it was like he was James Bond, she didn't believe he actually enjoyed it. He'd had his current glass all afternoon. "So what do you think about Nolan?" she asked.

"I'm not sure about the sales mafia thing. That was a bit out of left field."

"Yeah, he has some different ideas, he really wants to be a

disrupter. You know, come up with something that's never been done before."

"As long as he doesn't decide to disrupt us." Malcolm chuckled and pushed his glasses up. "I think he could work. He's definitely got the personality for it."

"Great, I can have Cheryl draw up a contract and we can see if we can get him on board next week. Hey, he could be a guest judge at the hackathon."

"Yeah, I guess it's definitely too late to get out of having a hackathon now."

"You're just suffering from 'not invented here'. You want everything to have come from you. You need to let the team come up with ideas. It gives them ownership."

"All the stock options we've given out gives them ownership. I don't need any new ideas, I need work done."

"Sometimes you need to let them create and design and have ideas of their own. And the best part is, if there is a great idea in there, it's still ours." She held up her drink for a toast. Malcolm complied, clinking his glass against hers.

"Hey!" complained Malcolm. "I did let them come up with the logo, and now we've got a small D". Gillian laughed.

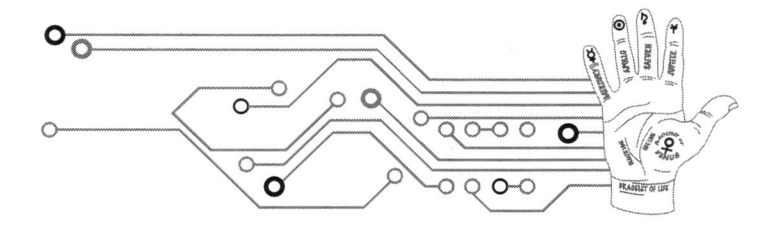

CHAPTER 0000 0011: THANKSGIVING

Raj sat by himself in the office on Monday. He was organizing the tasks he wanted to complete for the quarter, checking his tasks from the last quarter and comparing them against his goals for the year. This was how he got through his academic career, extreme organization. He spent 10 minutes meditating after everything was sorted. He liked it when he was in the office alone. Something about the large space and being by yourself made him calm. Halfway through his meditation he was distracted by the front door opening. Matt came strolling through the kitchen towards him. He was wearing a white shirt that said "Code until your fingers bleed" and had a stick figure with blood shooting out of its stumpy arms.

"I thought I'd find you here." Matt laughed.

"Shouldn't you be getting an overdose of tryptophan somewhere?" Raj asked him.

"Nah. The wife went to her family's place back east. She always tries to get away for hackathon week. So I'm doing the bachelor thing."

"I hear that." replied Raj.

"Whatcha doin'?"

"I was meditating until you came in. But, I'm organizing for next week and was just about to look into positive energy transference. I think it could be an idea for our hackathon project."

"Positive energy transference? What is that?" asked Matt. He pulled out the chair next to Raj and sat down. "Like positive thinking. I've read books on that."

Raj clicked away on his keyboard and pulled up a website. "Yes, it's like positive thinking. That's where I started. I've been trying to be more 'fun' lately, so I was reading the typical self-help mantras about being positive and then I hit on this one site that was about "Psi Programming for Positive Results". Obviously the term programming sucked me in. Then I stumbled on HSP or Higher Sense Perception."

Matt smiled, "What is it about programmers and three letter acronyms? They can't stay away from them."

"Right!" replied Raj. "So now I've gone down that rabbit hole so deep I was looking into whether positive thinking can cause positive energy and whether that energy could be transferred from one point to another." Raj looked at Matt, "Probably crazy, but you know how it goes once you get interested in something."

Matt nodded. He did know. That's how his life worked, jumping from one obsession to another. He found a lot of computer programmers were like that. "So you're thinking, Alice has positive thoughts, she creates an energy within herself and how can she beam it to Bob?"

"Not beam it like radio waves or something. On the website they talk about Alice hugging Bob or touching his arm or something, then Bob feels the positive energy."

"And then Bob can pass it on to Charlie?"

"I would assume so ..."

"Does it degrade as it is passed on?"

"Wow. OK, I'll send you the link to the website and you'll know as much as I do." Raj slid his mouse across the screen and opened up a private chat window.

"I wish I had brought my laptop in. This is interesting. If there is truly a signal of some sort that is "positive energy" then surely you could build something to detect it. I wonder if it emits a field of some sort like electricity. Then presumably you could get positive energy just by walking through the field."

"Maybe that's how people came up with the idea of Auras." Raj shrugged. He tilted his head to the side. "Originally I was just wondering if we could transfer it over some type of cabling, but if it does create a field you could potentially emit it from a device."

"Assuming there is such a thing as 'positive energy' and it's not just some basic human instinct to be happy around happy people."

"Truth. What we'd need first is a way to detect it." said Raj.

"I have to go get my laptop. I think we're starting hackathon early." Matt said as he jumped up from his chair and almost ran out the door.

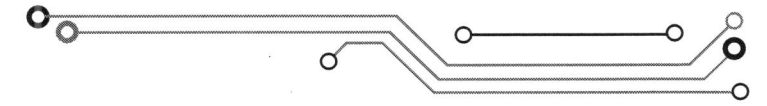

Malcolm was in his condo on a video chat with his parents. The laptop sat on an Ikea coffee table and he was sitting on the floor so he could still type without hunching over. His entire condo had been furnished from Ikea. He liked that look, he couldn't help it. He satisfied himself that he only bought the most expensive furniture they had, but in the end he knew his entire house looked like the showroom. Nobody really came over anyway, so he wasn't worried about it. Most of his friends were from work, so they met at the office or in a pub.

His mom was currently trying to show him their new pug "Walter". The dog was lucky his face was already so short as he was shoved into the camera so close Malcolm could only see one bulgy eye. Malcolm considered virtual calls great, he only had to switch to the video tab when they were showing him something. Otherwise he had a spreadsheet open and appeared to be staring diligently at his parents in Florida when he was actually going through the financials for the upcoming year.

"Well it sounds like this company is going to great, cybersecurity is all over the news down here." his dad was saying. Malcolm switched back to the video tab. His dad was looking older. He was still pretty fit, but the wrinkles seemed more pronounced now and his clothes fit him loose in the arms and shoulders. He was wearing a burgundy golf shirt that he got from one of the resorts down there. That's pretty much what he always had on. His thick white hair was slicked back the way he'd had it since the 60s and he perched his glasses on the end of his nose instead of getting bi-focals. "Once it takes off, maybe you can sell it and start thinking about a family."

This conversation had been done to death, Malcolm flipped back to his spreadsheet. "The company is my family dad. I'm happy where I am, I just want some credit for my work. Once this goes I'll be thinking about retirement, not a family."

His mom leaned forward. She had a habit of that, she thought the camera wouldn't pick her up if she was just sitting normally. Malcolm had tried to explain that she could see a preview of herself in the inset window but it never worked. She had cut her hair short after the move to Florida, Malcolm was still getting used to it. She had let it go grey as well, and it mostly was a pile on top of her head. Malcolm felt it made her look old. She didn't need glasses and Malcolm had always wished he had got her eyes. "Retirement? What would you do in retirement? Who would you spend all your time with?"

"I'd probably just sit on a few board of directors. Keep in the game so to speak. I'm thinking about learning to fly and sail."

"Well you have the money for it. I don't know why you don't just retire now then."

"Because I want to be a founder. I want my own company. To say 'I built that' and have a legacy."

"A legacy for who?" his mom questioned and leaned back into the couch. It was like she had just won some game. Malcolm sighed and switched back to the video screen.

"For the world mom. Living up to my potential and all that. Just like you guys always wanted." he reminded her.

"That was when you were in college." his dad said. "Now we just want you to be happy."

"Well I am happy. I truly am. I'm doing what I love and I love doing it. Adding anything else to my plate right now would just add stress and I'm sure you two don't want that."

Walter's rolled up tail went by the bottom of the screen and his parents glanced at each other. This was usually how it was. "Well, have a happy Thanksgiving, Malcolm. We're glad that you are loving what you do, just try something new once and while, maybe you'll find something else you love or maybe someone else …"

"Ok dad, I'll talk to you guys next week. Maybe I'll have something new going on then."

"Love you sweetie." said his mom as Malcolm moused over to the 'End Call' button. He could just barely hear "Wave Walter, wave goodbye" as the connection dropped.

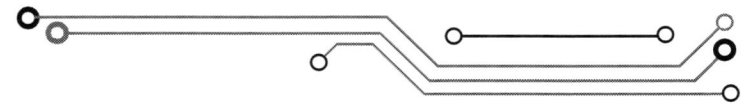

Gillian had driven back to Niagara to see her family for the long weekend. She loved the drive south from Waterloo. Cresting the top of the escarpment the sun was suddenly visible beyond the clouds above it. She felt like she was driving into a new world. Traffic was light and the Mazda was making good time. As she was driving over the Skyway, a large bridge over the Burlington Canal, she could look out at the lakefront and see a few boats with their sails out bobbing in the water.

She smiled to herself, someday she was going to move to a lakefront property. Maybe not in Burlington, but on Lake Huron or even up in the Muskokas. This was going to be her last tech company. She wanted a hobby farm, maybe with sheep and at least one horse. Once she had enough, she wanted to create art. She considered programming art as well, but she'd done that for so long she wanted a different outlet for her talents. Maybe even fashion. Heck, she thought, she could even open a flea market stall and just hang around on the weekends chatting with the other vendors about their knick knacks and antiquities.

Great, now she wanted to stop at a flea market. She laughed to herself. Maybe she'd make a quick stop at the one in Vineland as she passed by.

She wasn't worried about the financials from next year. She knew Nolan would do great and sales would start coming in. As much as Malcolm wanted to go public, Gillian figured she'd either sell her half to him before that or they'd accept an offer and get bought up by a larger enterprise. She was Ok with either one. Her exit strategy was the same. Travel for a bit and then settle down on that hobby farm. Life is good, she was thinking as she took the exit ramp in Vineland.

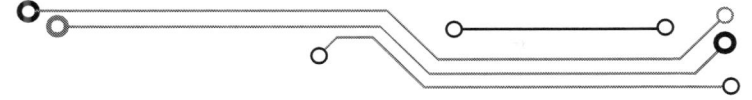

Jimmy had bought his parents house when they retired. And his parents hadn't left. He was comfortable in the basement and had converted most of it to server racks, desks and workbenches. He hated the thought of having to move his Bat-Cave anywhere and so had bought the house, and when his parents had asked if he was going to move to the main floor he answered with a flippant "Nah." So they had never moved out.

The only real home improvement he had done was to up the amperage that the electricity company ran to the house and add a noise filter on the line to protect his equipment. The basement had cable trays hanging from the ceiling that ran to server racks that were stacked against two walls. There was an electronics workbench against another wall that also served as the side table for his waterbed. The other side of the bed had his gaming table, with blue lights glowing beneath it and a water-cooled PC sitting on top. It was the only computer he didn't stick in a rack as he liked having his visitors ooh and ahh over it whenever they came in.

Jimmy himself was sitting in his pride and joy, the ErgoQuest Zero Gravity Workstation. It was a motorized recliner with 3 screens that mounted from arms that went over the top of the chair. He could recline the chair and the monitors would align themselves above him. It had a keyboard and mouse tray that rotated with the chair as well. He had paid well over ten thousand dollars for it and when he was coding at home, he barely left it.

He had a headset on and was talking to friends on Discord, an online voice chat site, about the problems with Google's latest open source software. One screen had an old Simpon's re-run going on it. Jimmy had watched every Simpson's TV show at least 3 times. A second screen was scrolling green text on black as he was re-installing some software for his server farm. The middle screen was open to a dark web chat site offering to sell credit card numbers for BitCoin.

He was tracking the usernames used in the chat and searching for the same username on other sites he used. Then he would link them together and build a profile of each user. This wasn't part of Jimmy's job, he just did it to help the community. He found attempting to track hackers' activity enjoyable and spent a lot of time doing it. It was like Oracle from Batman, always watching everything and doing anonymous good deeds. It always amazed him how little hackers hide their movements considering what they did.

A message popped up on his phone. "What hackathon team are you on?" It was Matt from work. He checked each of his screens to make sure things were still running then picked up his phone from the keyboard tray.

"w/sachet mike" he thumbed in quickly, dropped the phone on the tray and went back to his tracing.

A minute later the phone buzzed again. "Could you build this?" a photo came through of a whiteboard. The drawing on the whiteboard looked like a hockey helmet with squares sticking out of the top that were labelled 'Circuit Board'. The squares had cables, or least squiggly lines, that ran down to what looked like a network switch. Jimmy pushed a button on the arm of his chair and it slowly rotated down to a normal sitting position with a whir. With another push the monitors raised up out of the way. He picked up his phone and looked at the photo again, stretching it out on his phone with his fingers. It appeared to actually be a hockey helmet. It had circles drawn on the inside labelled 'heart monitor things'. Wires from these circles lead to another circuit board on the top of the helmet that had a doodle of some chips and components on it. Matt was never big on details, he was the big picture guy. He had drawn wires from the circuit board back to a box labelled "Magic".

"how?" he typed back. "dont knw what it is" He continued to stare at the drawing, wondering what Matt was up to now. Scanning brain waves maybe? He had heard of a few companies trying to do a direct brain to computer interface.

"Got time for a phone call?" came back the response.

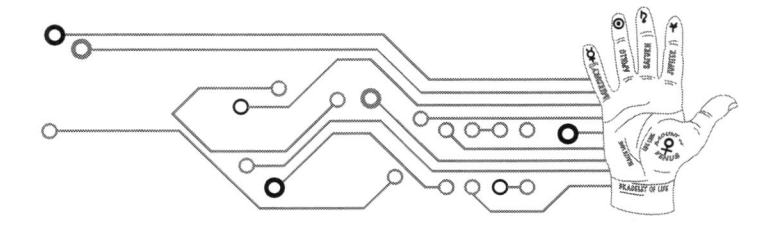

CHAPTER 0000 0100: HACKATHON

Tuesday woke up grumpy. The team was slowly filing into the office, most were still harbouring turkey hangovers from the day before. Cheryl put out the leftovers from her own Thanksgiving that she had brought in, but most of the team hardly touched them. Mike was an exception, he was coming into the kitchen area about once an hour and taking a small plate of pie or a Nanaimo bar from the spread laid out across the picnic tables. It was a grey drizzly day and no one was feeling like chatting. Most just sat at their desks working away and trying to file reports for the week since they'd be spending the rest of the week working on their hackathon projects.

Cheryl noticed one group was separated. Matt, Raj and Jimmy were tucked away on the couches in the corner of the open area whispering to each other with agitation and scribbling on a whiteboard. At lunch they all left together in Matt's car. Cheryl wondered what was going on.

After lunch Jimmy went into Mike's office and spoke with him for a short time. When he came out he headed straight over to Sachet's desk.

"Hey Sachet."

"Hey Jimmy, I'm glad you're here. I have an idea for our hackathon project."

"Actually," interrupted Jimmy, "that's what I'm here to talk about too. I'm afraid I've got involved with another team."

"What?" said Sachet, spinning in his chair to face Jimmy directly. He leaned back. "Are you having a dataffair?"

Jimmy laughed. "Yeah, I guess, something like that. Matt and Raj asked me for some help and I really got into what they're thinking." He stuffed his hands into his jean pockets and rocked on his feet.

"Ahh, that's ok." said Sachet, leaning forward again. "I had an idea where we could do facial recognition on customers' security cameras and then compare the faces to the staff list and alert on non-employees in the building."

"That's actually a cool idea," said Jimmy. He looked up at the ceiling, a sure sign that he was thinking. "I think you could actually do that, but I can't get into anything else right now. You'll have to wait and see why at the presentations. I already talked to Mike and he's good with it as well."

"I wondered what you guys were all talking about over there. I was worried that it was my test framework causing issues." Sachet managed to worry about everything. He even worried that he worried too much. One time when they were re-arranging the desks at the office, they had forgotten to put Sachet's name plaque back up and he assumed he had been fired.

"Nope. No worries. Wait until Friday. We'll either blow your mind, or you'll have a good laugh."

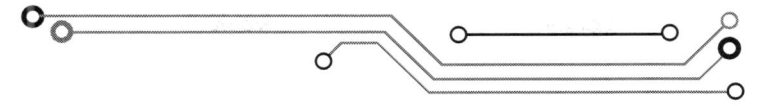

Raj and Matt had drawn up a circuit board that would mount on their hockey helmet. They were using an Arduino microcontroller that both had experience with. It was a small and inexpensive chip that both of them had laying around. They were using a Raspberry Pi in the "Magic" box, which was a tiny, inexpensive computer. For Hackathon it was perfect, it had USB ports, an HDMI port for a monitor connection and they could run any software they wanted without any issues.

They found they could get the sticky heart monitor pads online. They would use these to feed the positive energy they were attempting to collect back to the microcontroller. "Have you ever had those pads stuck to your chest?" Raj asked.

"No, why?" Matt retorted.

"They stick so well. When you take them off they rip the hairs right out of you." Raj was gesturing as though ripping his heart out of his chest. "Nobody is going to want that on their head. And for sure, no one is going to want to go second and have some sticker that looks like it just came out of a shower drain stuck on their head."

"Oh!" exclaimed Matt. "What if we stick them to loonies and then mount the coins into the inside of the helmet. Then they are reusable too."

"Good idea, but we should use the toonies, they have copper in the center inset, it would conduct things better."

"The cost of this project is doubling every minute!" laughed Matt.

Jimmy walked up to the whiteboard and surveyed it like he

was the final inspection before a rocket launch. He looked at the circuit board with it's amplifier, diodes, and resistors and traced the circuits that led to the microcontroller and to the "Toonie" nodes. "What makes you think all this positive energy is going to come from the head?" he asked out loud.

Matt and Raj looked at each other with raised eyebrows.

"I mean, in your description you mentioned a hug," continued Jimmy, "What if it comes out everywhere, or it's just like an aura that surrounds you."

"Good point." said Matt and stared at the circuit board as well. "But if it comes out everywhere, then we're still OK getting it from the head. I guess we could build a whole positivity suit if we wanted."

"Hmmm" hummed Raj, staring at the whiteboard.

"Well I need to finish my reports," said Jimmy, "Or else I'm not going to get to participate in hackathon. I'll see if I can etch this board tonight. I have an extra Raspberry Pi we can use and lots of Arduino's. Something to think about if we don't get the results we expect. Who's writing the software to isolate the energy?"

"I'm going to write that. Started it last night." said Raj with a smile of pride. "Tonight I'm going to write the filters to get rid of the actual brain activity and heartbeat interference, things like that. It should be easy to filter them out, I expect them to be much stronger and consistent."

"Cool." Jimmy said. He pulled out his phone and began taking pictures of the whiteboard.

"And I'm writing up a user interface to graph out the energy that we detect, give us a visual of it so to speak." added Matt.

"Nice. This is going to be something if it actually works. Maybe not sellable, but something." he laughed.

"Yeah, we're not sure how to tie it to cybersecurity yet or DAYtaffair." Matt had begun over pronouncing the 'Day' portion of Dataffair since the episode with Sachet. It was quickly becoming annoying and both Raj and Jimmy rolled their eyes.

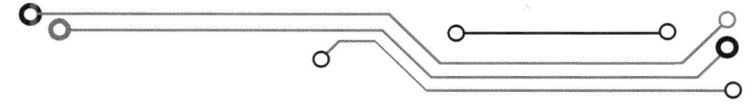

Wednesday came out of nowhere. The Dataffair office sounded like it had 3 times as many staff as it did. There was the smell of chocolate chip muffins in the air that Cheryl had brought in for breakfast and the kitchen was literally sizzling as she made sausage, bacon and pancakes for everyone. Gillian and Malcolm were both in and enjoying breakfast at one of the picnic tables. Malcolm had still brought his coffee in, but Gillian was drinking the office coffee from a cup with an earlier version of the Dataffair logo on the side. Hackathon teams had grouped together at the tables and discussion was loud and frantic. Malcolm could overhear ideas for new data rules, increased monitoring, and new ways to track data migration within a company to find employees that were exfiltrating secrets outside the company. He thought he heard something about network attached extra-sensory perception, but assumed it was part of a joke.

Gillian had her laptop open and was scrolling through her emails slowly as she had to put her fork down each time to touch the trackpad. "Oh" she suddenly exclaimed around a stick of bacon she was just putting in her mouth. "We got a response from Nolan. It looks like he's taking the contract, no changes."

"Yes!" exclaimed Malcolm, making a fist with one hand. "Here comes the sales train."

"Correction, here comes the sales mafia," said Gillian raising her coffee mug.

Malcolm hoisted his in the toast and said "We should announce this to the team. Oh wait. We should see if he wants to be a guest judge for the hackathon first, so we can announce both things at lunch."

"Ohhh, good idea." replied Gillian. She pulled her laptop closer to her, pushing her plate out of the way, and began her response. "I'll ask him right now. I can ask him to bring in the signed papers then too."

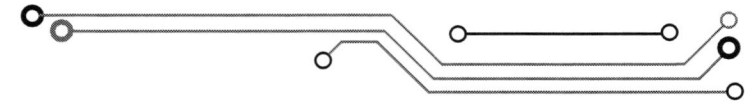

Team Psi Phi made up of Matt, Raj and Jimmy were not at one of the picnic tables. The trio had filled a plate with bacon and breakfast sausages, and another with sections of pineapple, melon, and apple. They had asked Mike to borrow his office and had been resident there since they arrived. If they had brought 3 chairs in, they wouldn't have had any room, but only Raj was sitting anyway. The other two paced behind him. Mike had an L shaped desk that wrapped around two walls. One side had Raj's laptop open and he had connected it to Mike's 2 other monitors so everyone could see what he was working on. The corner of the L had a charcoal coloured, metal box on it that was not very high, but wide. It had ports across the front for connecting more cables and one of these cables ran to Raj's computer. The rest ran down the other desk to a white, dinged up, hockey helmet covered in multi-coloured wires with a blue circuit board mounted on top. Beside it was a hot glue gun plugged into the wall and soldering iron resting in its spring-like stand.

Jimmy was fiddling with the connections to the circuit board. "This thing needs a name." he said aloud as he pushed a connector in deeper. He flipped the helmet over to look at the inside and placed it back down on the desk.

"Oh gawd." muttered Matt. "Computer people shouldn't name things. We should let Andrea name it after we win."

"After we win." repeated Jimmy. "I like that." He grabbed the glue gun and began mounting toonies into sockets he had cut out of the inside styrofoam padding with an exacto knife. Each toonie had a node already connected to it that ran through holes that had been drilled through plastic of the helmet.

"I vote for Positron, Healer of Worlds" said Raj without looking away from his code.

"You're just going to write out the various signals as a comma separated file right?" asked Matt looking over Raj's shoulder and ignoring the naming idea.

"Yes there will be a value for each sensor per row, unless we don't receive anything, then it will be null."

"Ok, perfect, how many sensors are we putting in Jimmy and I'll go finish up the graphing portion of the code."

"I'm mounting eight." replied Jimmy. "But I'm leaving two dangling as well in case we want to check other spots on the body," he added quietly. He had to talk with his tongue stuck out since he was focused so directly on getting the coin to fit exactly in the niche cut out for it.

"You're going to stick one on your butt, eh?" said Matt shaking his head as he opened the office door.

"You know it!" shouted Jimmy at his back.

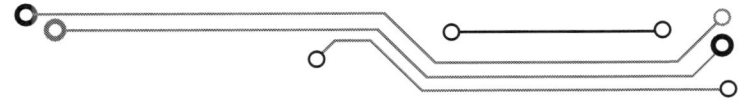

Matt walked through the open area grabbing his laptop as he passed his desk. He took it into the kitchen and put it down on the picnic table beside Gillian. "Mind if I join you guys?" he asked before climbing onto the bench.

"For sure." responded Gillian. "What are you guys working on? Seems exciting."

"Top secret I'm afraid, but I promise you it will be the most interesting project you see." Matt said with his eyebrows raised. Malcolm couldn't tell if he was being sarcastic or not. "What are you guys talking about?" Matt asked.

"Looks like Nolan is accepting our offer," said Malcolm.. "Gillian is going to see if he wants to be a guest judge for the hackathon while he's in town."

"Nice." commented Matt. "And who else is going to judge?" he asked, looking back and forth between the two founders.

"Well we tried to get Elon Musk and Bill Gates." joked Gillian.

"Unfortunately one is going to space this week and the other is starting a competing business, so we didn't feel comfortable with them poking around." muttered Malcolm.

"But we did get a couple of really good ones. Keep this under your hat," whispered Gillian leaning closer to Matt, "but we managed to get the Mayor, John Dickinson for the innovation side of things and Bev Shepherd from NextGig to judge the tech side. Combine that with Nolan for the sales side and I think we did pretty awesome."

Malcolm commented "And we've kept everything at arms length, no worries about playing favourites."

"Bev Shepherd!" whispered Matt excitedly. "How did we get her? Isn't she doing angel investing out in Vancouver?"

"I actually met her on a panel for Code Like A Girl," said Gillian. "I couldn't believe it when she accepted. She said hackathons are right up her alley. She loves seeing new ideas before they are fleshed out and things like cost and margins start forcing them to reduce to base principles. She flies in tomorrow night."

"Wow. That's amazing. I'd love to get a chance to talk to her.

I feel like NextGig kickstarted the gig economy." He paused for a moment, looking at a private chat message from Raj. "So back to Nolan though, when do we see the first sale?" he asked.

"Once we get some paperwork out of the way he's good to go. I imagine it will take him a while to get running." answered Gillian. "I'm excited to see what he can do though. He worked for me before and it didn't take long till he had a team together and sales started coming in." Malcolm wasn't paying attention anymore. He had this vision in his head of the Sales Mafia extorting cybersecurity services from small businesses. In his mind they all wore the 1920's suits with fedoras and talked like cartoon gangsters. 'I'd hate to see all this data go missing.' the gangster muttered in his head, patting a USB key in his pocket, adding 'It would sure be a shame if a nice company like yours winds up with the ransomwares.' Malcolm shook the thought out of his head and noticed both Matt and Gillian were looking at him.

"What's that?" he asked, his eyes opening wider.

"I was just asking if you had done sales for any of your previous companies." Matt said, looking at Malcolm expectantly.

"Oh yeah, but totally not my thing." said Malcolm, pushing back his hair. "When I was at UnWare I went on a bunch of sales calls in the beginning. I have no problem with the stats and selling the numbers, but just couldn't connect with the customers. I realized quickly that these relationship building jobs weren't for me. If anything I could see Gillian doing a much better job."

"Oh no." Gillian laughed. "I've done sales for a few startups and it definitely isn't for me. I can make the connection, but I can't put on the pressure. They say 'No' and I'm back in my car calling my Mom to cry." She made a fake pout and then laughed again.

"Aww, muffin." said Matt sarcastically, "Well then I'm glad we're bringing Nolan on board, 'cause it sounds like you both suck." He laughed and turned to his laptop. "Ok, I need to get this interface done to blow your minds in 2 days."

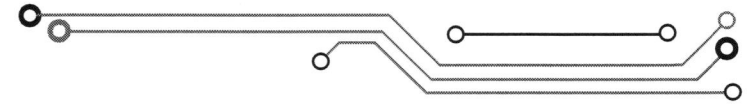

Jimmy had the hockey helmet on his head, the wires stuck out in all directions and the straps hung down around his shoulders. He found the weight of the circuit board did nothing to affect the fit. He could feel one coin digging into his forehead a bit. "I feel like we need to 3D print a holder for these front coins. Then they could rest flat against the forehead. Oh!" he exclaimed. "Make them adjustable as well. Raise and lower. We should totally put that on a servo so they are automatic, Iron Man style."

Raj spun his chair around and surveyed Jimmy's head. He looked like a low-budget sci-fi film extra. "We should spray paint it. And add some lights to make it more technical looking." he said putting his hand on his chin and crossing his legs. "This looks too easy, we need to make it look more complicated."

"Good idea." said Jimmy with excitement. "I can add a bunch of old stuff I've got at home. Maybe some vacuum tubes and retro shit." he added, taking off the helmet. "We could make it look like it's right of the Star Wars set."

"Nice." said Raj, nodding his head. "People love that. Presentation is just Invention in the Present."

Jimmy looked up from the helmet at Raj with his eyebrows bunched and mouth in a grimace. "What? That doesn't work."

"Hey, I'm trying some new material." shrugged Raj and spun his chair back around. Jimmy shook his head and put the helmet down on the desk. He peered at the screen over Raj's shoulder and twisted his mouth. Assuming any kind of signal came out of their device, it looked like this would work. Raj's code was always so eloquent, it was like reading a poem except every line had a comment to tell you what it meant. The algorithms were set out and easy to identify and no code was ever duplicated. Jimmy admired code like that even though he never bothered to write like that himself. He was more a pulp fiction writer. Get it done and get it live.

They continued to work heads down until they heard Cheryl call for the lunch break.

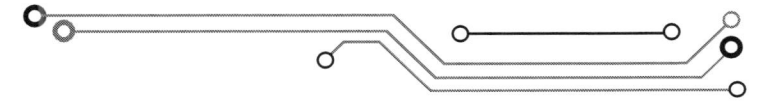

Malcolm and Gillian stood by the reception area. Malcolm was checking his phone as everyone filed through the buffet line of cold cuts and sandwiches. The spread was laid out across the laminate kitchen counters and everyone was filling a plate and taking a seat at the tables. Gillian was watching the team, excited to make the announcement of who would be judging the hackathon. She was getting nostalgic about when it was just her and Malcolm chatting at the Code and Clam, deciding to start a new company. After getting their initial investments settled between them they had quickly grabbed this space and ramped up to the team they had now.

That was over a year ago now and they were just getting started. She wasn't sure she wanted to ride this rollercoaster again. It was amazing the difference a year made. Either way she was happy right now with this team and how things were moving forward.

"Ok everyone." she shouted over the crowd noise. "We have a couple of announcements and then we'll let you get back to your projects. I'm sure most of you are past the idea phase and starting to get things going." There were a few groans throughout the tables.

"First off, a huge thanks to Cheryl for that amazing breakfast." This led to a round of applause and Cheryl blushing and waving from the back. Gillian applauded herself and gestured towards the buffet. "And a second thanks for this great lunch buffet. I know I've been picking at the olives for the last hour." There was another burst of cheers and clapping that tapered off. Malcolm put his phone in his pocket to join in and survey the room.

"Ok, now for the big news. The judges for Friday are confirmed and we are ready to let you know who they are." Everyone turned to face her expectantly. She could see the anticipation on their faces. Hopefully they found the news as exciting as she did.

"First, we have Nolan Walker, who will be our brand new VP of sales." Light applause.

"Second, we have John Dickinson, mayor of the City of Waterloo." Slightly larger applause.

"And in case of a tie, we have Bev Shepherd of NextGig joining us as well." She could hear some gasps and someone said "Oh my gawd" very loudly, then the applause really broke out.

"Nolan will be looking for a sellable product, the mayor will be looking for innovation and Ms. Shepherd will be looking at the technical execution of your projects." The team was already talking amongst themselves, whispering about how cool it was going to be to meet Bev Shepherd. Malcolm was smiling. He loved it when the team was excited, they did great work when they were engaged like that.

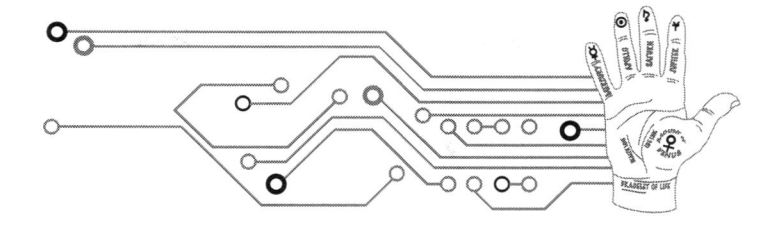

CHAPTER 0000 0101: HACKATHON 2.0

Thursday was eager to get started. Jimmy was the first to arrive, carrying his newly updated hockey helmet carefully in both hands. He used his hip to push the automatic door opener at the front and then used his foot to push the door open faster. He hit the light switch with his elbow and did his best fast walk back to Mike's office. As he cleared the open area he noted Nasser sleeping on the couches in the corner. "Rough night buddy?" he shouted over to him.

Nasser turned and rolled to face the back of the couch. "So many rules. So many beers." he mumbled and plumped up the sofa cushion he was using as a pillow before dropping his head back down.

Jimmy carefully placed the helmet on the desk in Mike's office. He was truly impressed with what he had accomplished last night. He couldn't wait for the others to get in and see it. 3D printed arms were now attached to the front of the helmet and came down to fit squarely against the wearer's head. Jimmy had taken advantage of the mounts for the visor to print another curved bar that attached to the arms and was used to raise and lower them using a motor mounted over the ear cover. He had wired the motor up to the microcontroller board so that it could be raised and lowered remotely.

A black triangular antennae came up from the side now. It served absolutely no purpose, but he felt like it made the user look more like Bobba Fett from Star Wars. Blue LED lights mounted between the padding now lit the head of the user in an extraterrestrial glow that made the user almost look angelic. The lights dimmed when no signal was being received and glowed brighter as the signal increased.

He suddenly noted that Nasser was leaning against the door jamb of the office. "What the hell is that?" Nasser yawned.

"Hey, hey!" shouted Jimmy. "No peeking until the big reveal tomorrow."

"Sure, sure." Nasser muttered, shuffling back out towards the kitchen. "I need to get a coffee anyway."

"Good plan. I'll join you." said Jimmy, closing the door as he headed towards the kitchen as well.

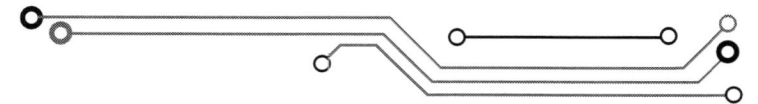

Raj was just coming into the kitchen as Nasser and Jimmy walked into it. "Did you sleep in your clothes?" he asked Nasser, giving him a look of contempt. Raj was in khaki pants with a black belt that had a buckle that was so shiny it looked like it was still shrink wrapped. He had a freshly ironed, short sleeved dress shirt in gray and his hair was perfect.

"Hey, they were good enough for yesterday, they are good enough for today." replied Nasser not even looking at Raj but instead focusing on getting the coffee maker running.

"Jimmy, I've got some new code we need to load onto the

microcontroller right away. Wait till you see what I wrote last night." Raj said excitedly as he slung his laptop back off his shoulder. "I think we'll be able to ..."

"Shhh, shhh." hushed Jimmy, putting his finger to his lips. "The competition is standing right here."

Nasser laughed. "I don't know what you guys are doing, but I can tell you that thanks to Jimmy-boy here I've picked up Sachet on our team and we're building something very cool." He swiveled his head as he talked like he was swishing around an idea.

"The facial recognition thing?" asked Jimmy.

"Ah, Sachet!" cried Nasser.

Jimmy put his still empty mug on the counter. "I'll be back." he proclaimed as he and Raj headed for Mike's office. Once they were safely ensconced inside with the door closed, Jimmy began prying the microcontroller from it's socket on top of the helmet. "What do you have for us, your pre-emminence?" he asked.

"Well, we wanted to separate expected signals from our other energy signatures right? So I was testing actually reading in the heart rate and brain activity on their own feed and then just subtracting that from the overall signal. Then we would have a live feed to adjust the calculations, and it totally worked." exclaimed Raj in one long breath.

"So our filter is dynamic now?" asked Jimmy. "Like if the user's brain activity changes, we automatically update the filter. That's sweet." Raj was always impressed by Jimmy's ability to pick up on things like that. Even though Jimmy didn't have the education, his natural intelligence got him through. Raj often wondered if he hadn't had the massive amount of education he went through would he have the same deductive reasoning Jimmy did.

"Exactly." he said, setting up his laptop and connecting all the cables to it. "Hopefully Matt has an interface for us and we're not just trying to look at a stream of numbers, but I think we're ready for test zero."

"And test zero is ...?" asked Jimmy.

"Someone puts it on and we see if anything happens. Wow!" he exclaimed as he noticed the helmet for the first time. "That's amazing! We should win just for the coolest looking accessory." He stared at it for a while, then suddenly realized something. "Oh yeah, I used those two extra leads for the heart and brain filter."

"What?" Jimmy whined, "but I was going to use them."

"Yeah, to find signals from Uranus!" Raj exploded. "We're looking for positive energy, not trying to solve the mysteries of Jimmy's ass." he was shaking the two leads in Jimmy's face.

"Ok, ok." said Jimmy raising his hands in defence. "After the hackathon I can try to solve that mystery. I would've totally gotten away with it too, if it wasn't for you kids." The two smirked and Raj connected the cables from the helmet to the magic box. "So once we get the signal, then we still need to attempt to send it somewhere and see if it affects anything."

"Yes, and building another Positron, Healer of Worlds is too much to do, with only one day left in the hackathon. I'm hoping we can build an insulated box and then just use a few of the extra heart monitors we have to read any changes inside the box to see if our signal actually transferred to the box or the whole thing is a load of shit and we should've joined Sachet's team and done the facial recognition thing."

The door opened and Matt popped his head in. "Safe to come in?" His shirt read "Keep Your Bits Clean" with a series of ones and zeros that appeared to be rusting..

Jimmy turned to him, "I'm just going to run home and build a

Faraday cage." he said. "Don't turn anything on until I get back." Matt could feel a breeze as Jimmy rushed past him.

"Faraday cage?" he questioned Raj, "Sounds like a hardware problem."

"It is." replied Raj, "It'll block any external signals from interfering with our readings when we try to actually send the signal to a remote location."

"Cool," said Matt. "And thinking of cool, wait until you see this interface. Whoa wait!" Matt noticed the helmet on the desk. "That looks amazing. Are those lights inside it?" he asked as he slipped his own backpack off and put it on the desk beside the helmet.

"Yes they are!" Raj said with enthusiasm. "Jimmy has outdid himself on this one. The frontal sensors raise and lower with this motor as well."

Matt was pulling out his laptop and opening it while still admiring the helmet. "This is definitely going to be over the top. What's the antenna piece for?" he asked.

"No idea …" said Raj, looking at the black triangular monolith jutting from the side of the helmet.

Matt logged into his computer and opened up a browser tab. "Now this is just sample data of course, I didn't have any real data to work with." he said as he began leading Raj through the various graphs and dashboards he had created the night before.

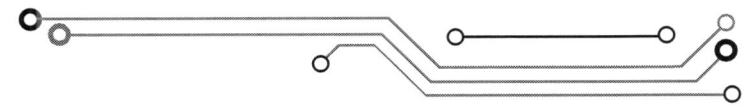

Malcolm felt good this morning. He had done a 5k run before showering and dressing for work. When he arrived everyone was busy, just the way he liked it. Gillian was sitting at a picnic table talking to Nasser, who appeared to be in the same clothes as yesterday based on the number of wrinkles in them. "Hey guys." he said as he laid his backpack on the table. "Grabbing a coffee and I'll be back." They made non-committal greetings and continued their conversation. Sachet was at the coffee maker.

"How's the project coming?" Malcolm asked as he approached.

Sachet looked up from his coffee mug. He had been deep in thought. "Oh, hey Malcolm. Not bad. Mike's working remotely because he said he needs his private space. Nasser joined us and we made some serious progress yesterday, but then we stayed a bit late and enjoyed some of the libations left out." he made a sad laugh.

Malcolm laughed and started making his own coffee. "Oh God, who did this?" he asked. The coffee maker's display, which usually showed how long the pot had been on, was slowly scrolling "Don't feed the staff, they may start to rely on it."

Sachet watched it scroll by, "Huh," he said, "I never even noticed that ..."

Malcolm sighed. "What are you guys working on? You can tell me, I'm not judging this year."

"We're trying to set up facial recognition on a security camera and then compare the faces to the company directory. When a non-employee enters the scene, bam, an alert goes out that there is someone in the building."

"Interesting." said Malcolm putting his hand on his chin and thinking about it. "What if they have a guest, is that going to continuously alert? Like when we had Nolan in last week."

"On the first alert, IT can silence it by adding the face to the database with an expiry date, so the alerts will start again after that time." Sachet was getting more excited as he talked and appeared to perk up. These kinds of conversations always made Malcolm feel like he was a good boss. Listening to his employees and asking questions that showed he was interested in what they were talking about.

"Well done, I like it. I need to talk to Gillian, but good luck, can't wait to see what you have tomorrow." he turned to walk back to the picnic tables.

As he approached the table Nasser was getting up from it awkwardly and slowly. "I better go help Sachet. We're not sure what Mike is doing and the rest of the team mutinied. They still wanted to write the new dark web rules so we let them make a new team."

Malcolm put his coffee down and squeezed into the bench across from Gillian. "Did you hack the coffee machine last night?" he asked.

Nasser started to get up faster, "Someone hacked the coffee machine? That's terrible ..." he said quickly as he left.

"So I got an email from Nolan this morning." Malcolm said as he pulled his backpack over to him and unzipped it.

"He's not backing out is he?" she asked closing her own laptop screen part way to remove the distraction just as Malcolm was opening his up.

"No no. Better than that. He's set up a sales meeting with a law firm in town."

"No way!" Gillian exclaimed. "That's amazing."

"Apparently, a client from a previous company, so he took advantage of his stay here to set things up. He wants the two of us to attend though, he says it will bring more credibility to the table."

"I can do that." Gillian responded. "Especially to get our first sale, I take it this is a direct sale and not through a service provider?"

"Yes, direct to the customer. Gives us some wiggle room on pricing as well without the middle man. We're going to meet their vice president of IT directly. Apparently she has the budget and signing authority to make it happen right then and there."

"This is so good," said Gillian. "You aren't stressing about a sales call are you?"

"A little. First one, we don't know what data they'll be looking for, how we fit into their needs and it's the litmus test to see if what we built is what customers want. We'll need to set expectations appropriately." said Malcolm. "This is good though. It's the beginning of a whole new era for Dataffair."

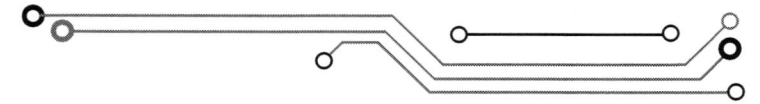

Jimmy was back at the office by 2:00 in the afternoon. He had with him a box about the size of his chest. It was made out of cardboard and covered in silver duct tape. He had lined the inside with a mesh of copper wire and left a flap that opened to place the sensors inside. Matt and Raj were glad to see him. They had all of their equipment set up and were eagerly awaiting the final piece. Jimmy had used a permanent marker to write "Danger: Extreme Positivity" on the outside of the box in big block letters.

"Ok" exhaled Matt. "I think we are ready for a trial run." He rubbed his hands together in excitement. "We're going to need a baseline, so who do we think is the median of positivity between us?" he asked.

Raj and Jimmy both looked at each other, then at Matt. Matt held out his hands and looked from Raj to Jimmy. He could tell what they were thinking. "Got it," he said and picked up the helmet. Raj connected a network cable to the magic box with a click. He ran the other end into the Faraday cage and plugged it into their sensor. He pulled up Matt's user interface on one of the mounted monitors. The dashboard showed a bar graph in one corner of the current signal coming in from each node. The bars began to move up and down slightly as the signals fluctuated. A second graph beside it showed a line graph of each signal over time. They could see that the signals were changing, but only slightly, nothing significant.

"Each of our sensors is on a different line." said Raj pointing at the graph. "Currently we are seeing less than 1% variation. It's interesting. We aren't seeing a change in the total of all signals at all. If one goes down another goes up. Whatever this signal is," Raj pointed at one of the lines that was higher than the rest, "it's the predominant value right now. Wonder what it is."

Jimmy and Matt were staring at the screen intently watching the lines move slowly up and down with each reading. Matt still had the helmet in his hands and slowly raised it up and pulled it over his head. "Ready," he said.

Raj stood and grabbed the two leads for the filter that were dangling down in front of Matt. He pulled the front of Matt's shirt down and placed one on his chest, securing it with an adhesive bandage. He attached the other sensor to the side of Matt's head the same way. Turning and lowering himself into the chair he clicked a button on the dashboard and the front levers of the helmet lowered until they were pressed against Matt's forehead. A blue glow began to form on his rusty hair from inside the helmet. The light leaked out through the slats in the headgear and began to pulse in a rhythmic way. Jimmy's eyes got wide as he watched. "It's working." he whispered as though a sudden noise would spoil the effect. The three had their eyes glued to the monitor and watched the lines start to shift. The value that was already high began to rise even higher and the others began to sink.

"Annotating helmet contact." said Raj as he right clicked on the graph creating a vertical line marking the point when the helmet had been placed on Matt's head. "We are still seeing a steady aggregate across all values." One bar on the graph was now obviously way larger than the others as those sank to almost nothing. "Something is definitely happening." squealed Raj. "This is amazing. But what is it?"

Movement on the line graph was dominated by a single blue streak. All were breathless as it climbed and then began to level out. "Maybe it's just nervous energy." said Matt, "This is kind of freaking me out."

"No," answered Raj, "the filter would be eliminating that. We are definitely reading something."

"There's one way to find out." said Jimmy and flung his fist backwards into Matt's groin.

"WHAT THE FUCK!" screamed Matt clutching his crotch with both hands. Immediately the line on the graph that had been so high dropped to nothing. It looked like it would plunge past the zero point and wind up coming out the bottom of the monitor. Another line, bright green, shot up taking over the entire chart. Raj jumped out of his chair throwing his hands in the air.

"It's working!" he shouted.

"Couldn't we have done that in a way that doesn't involve me filing a report with HR" Matt groaned.

"Sorry about that." said Jimmy patting Matt on the back, "It just popped into my head and I flinched."

"Oh? Flinched? That makes me feel better." cried Matt sarcastically. They all turned as there was a knock on the office door. It opened a bit and Cheryl's head appeared inside.

"Are you guys ok?" she asked. Raj jumped in front of the screen blocking it with his body before realizing Cheryl would have no idea what they were doing. Anyway, she was staring at Matt's helmet with questions all over her face.

"Yeah, we're ok, sorry about the outburst," replied Matt. He noticed that Cheryl made a distinct look at his hands, which were clenched around his groin, holding himself, and quickly added "Oh yeah, I think my vasectomy stitches let go."

Cheryls eyes became huge. "Oh." she said in a whisper. "Ok then, well, if you need anything ..." she left off, pulling her head back through the door, closing it slowly behind her.

"I didn't know you had a vasectomy," said Jimmy.

"I didn't, until now maybe." rasped Matt, "I had to say something to explain why I'm grabbing my bits in an office with two coworkers."

"Keep 'em clean," winked Jimmy.

Matt finally got a chance to look at the dashboard on Raj's screen. "So what does this mean exactly? It detected pain?"

"Well," started Raj, "I'm hoping this signal is the negative energy and the line that dropped was the positive energy. See how the blue is starting to rise above zero again, and the green is now starting to drop. I suppose it could be pain." he scratched his hair, then patted it back down to perfection. "We'll have to run some tests and see if we can determine what each of these signals are."

"The data for each line could be coming from a single sensor or it could be coming from all of them," Matt remarked. "Once the signal runs through your filtering, I look for patterns in the noise and then lock those to a single line. I could have it display which sensors it winds up with once it's locked onto a certain pattern."

"I think that would be interesting," added Raj, "but it would be strictly academic if we are getting the data we want. I think we just need to isolate which of the lines is which. Can you think of something happy?"

"Like what?"

"I don't know, anything happy. Maybe the time just before

Jimmy sacked you?"

"That was a happier moment in my life." muttered Matt as he gave Jimmy a glare.

"I apologized!" cried Jimmy.

"Ok, I'm going to think happy thoughts now." Matt closed his eyes and attempted to focus on the birth of his first child. He remembered the first cry, the slow drive home, the first smile, gas or not. He found himself not wanting to open his eyes. He missed his kids and was excited to have them back this weekend when his wife arrived home.

"Happy line going back up!" cried Jimmy. "That's definitely the happy line. Positive energy baby! We have a box full of positive energy!" Jimmy began a little shuffle on the carpet. "Wait." he stopped. "How do we know this is actually coming from Matt's head? I mean, we don't even know if a Faraday cage would block positive energy, so even if we are properly sensing it, it could just be travelling across the room."

"Interesting." nodded Raj. "We need a longer cable."

"There's a box of cable in the server room, I'll go grab it and crimp some ends on." boomed Jimmy and flung open the door. They watched him walk quickly across the open area and then turned back to the screens. Raj sat at the keyboard and labelled the blue line 'Happy'. He labelled the green line 'Grumpy' and Matt laughed. The happy line immediately went higher and grumpy sank lower towards zero.

"Wow. This seriously seems to be working." whispered Matt, watching the lines with intensity.

"Jimmy is right though," remarked Raj. "There are people detecting emotions from facial expressions using AI. Essentially this is just the same thing unless we can actually capture the emotion and send it over a distance."

"What are these other lines though? Seems like we got the simple ones, but the others are all so small, they could be anything." Matt wondered. "My code may even be combining unrelated emotions if that's what they are. Sadness and anger may be grouped together, pride and empathy could be the same even."

"I think ideally we want only two lines. Positive and Negative. Maybe you need to loosen the restrictions in your code to allow it to group them one way or the other. So sadness and anger both go to negative and pride and empathy both go to positive. That would certainly make it easier to explain when we demo it tomorrow."

"Good idea. And an easy change to make, I put the sensitivity into a configuration file since I assumed we'd be tweaking it as we went." Matt took off the helmet and laid it on the desk. He noted that the lines began to converge at one point on the graph. "That's amazing." he said as he opened his laptop to work.

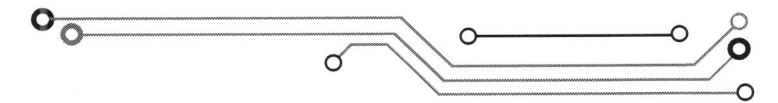

Gillian was preparing a slide deck for the sales meeting. She sat at one of the kitchen picnic tables. Malcolm was at another table with his glasses off massaging the bridge of his nose with two fingers. He put his glasses back on and went back to furiously typing on his keyboard. Tomorrow would be busy with the hackathon judging and she didn't like giving up her weekend for the company. She knew Malcolm would be working on the slides the whole time, so she thought she'd give him a head start. Andrea had already prepared a template so it was mostly filling in the text, adding some charts and getting a good flow to the presentation. She had called Nolan to see if he had any ideas, but she was pretty sure he didn't even know what he was really selling. He had told her "Does a high jumper know what the bar is made of? No. Who cares? As long as you get over it, you win. Like I said, I'm in the business of selling, not what I'm selling." This didn't make her feel any better. She hoped he didn't repeat it to Malcolm. She was happy though, the Log Driver product was good and a law firm was a perfect fit. They needed cybersecurity to protect the privacy of their clients. All of the data they stored could be leaked to the public if ever there was a breach of their network.

Even though she didn't want to spend all her time working, it was work that she enjoyed. She felt like they were not just building something, but helping people to stay safe. It was unfortunate that there was something to stay safe from. She never understood why someone would purposely steal information, sometimes for money, sometimes just for the fun of it and leak private information. It was like going through someone's purse. And these weren't exactly the poor and destitute. Any hacker could make a good living programming or working in IT. They didn't need to hack, but for some reason their ethics weren't aligned, or they couldn't see how it affected people. During her career she'd seen a lot of lives turned upside down from stolen identities and data.

She was concerned as she was writing up the slides about fear mongering. She didn't want to come across as aggressive, obviously she wouldn't fit in the sales mafia. She was lost in thought as she watched Jimmy half jog across the kitchen and badge into the server room. She wondered what that team was working on this year. They'd been cooped up in Mike's office so long and no one was spilling the beans on what they were doing. She was still working on the slides when Jimmy emerged with a 1,000 foot box of network cable with the two ends crimped and dangling from the box. She cocked her head to the side as he shut the door and quickly walked past her. She looked at Malcolm, but he hadn't even raised his head, apparently deep into whatever he was working on. Well at least the project had something to do with networking, she thought and returned to working on the slides.

After a few minutes Matt walked into the kitchen backwards, wearing what was apparently a helmet for hockey in outer space. He was carrying his laptop balanced on one hand and had a device box of some sort in the other. A cable was dragging behind him that led back into the open area. He continuously glanced behind him as he walked through the kitchen, out the reception and exited through the glass doors. She watched him pass the windows outside until he stooped to apparently plug in his box to an outdoor receptacle. He then stood staring into the window, apparently looking through to Mike's office. He gave an OK sign through the window, then noticed her watching. He smiled and waved. She waved back. This is what she loved about startups she thought. You just never know what's going to happen next.

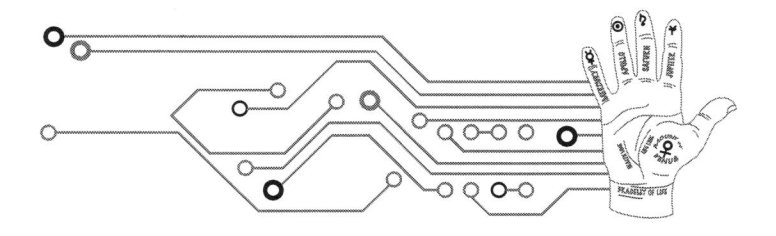

CHAPTER 0000 0110: DEMO DAY

Jimmy saw the OK sign from Matt outside. This was a real test. Could he affect the energy in the box from a distance? In the tech world "spooky action at a distance" was usually considered a bad thing, but this was different. "He's ready," he said to Raj and closed the door to the office. He rubbed his hands together as he looked at the lines on the screen. There were now only two, one labelled 'Happy' and the other 'Grumpy'. They had changed the axis to a percentage since the total energy didn't appear to change. Happiness was at 60% and grumpy was sitting at 40%. Jimmy was thinking how much easier it would be during the hiring process if they could detect 'Dopey' and smiled to himself.

Raj placed his phone on the desk beside his laptop. He punched Matt's contact and then the speaker button. It rang once before Matt's voice came on. "I'm ready. What do you want me to do?"

"We're all set in here." said Raj, "Let's start with something simple. Try to send positive thoughts our way."

Matt thought about doing the same thing as last time, but then figured he should change it up. See what kind of thoughts project positive energy into the universe. He thought about his University graduation. His parents were both alive, everyone seemed happy then. The entire extended family all met in his home town of Barrie the next day for a huge bash to celebrate the completion of his first degree. What an amazing time.

Inside the office Raj whispered, "Matt is now entering the cosmic realm. His thoughts are being read by the Positron and sent down hundreds of feet of cable, manifesting themselves here. It's amazing and a bit beautiful." They were watching the happy line climb to the top of the chart as the grumpy line sank.

Jimmy also had his eyes on the screen and was thinking about what Raj said, then suddenly interjected "So what?".

Happy line began to drop and Matt's voice came over the phone, "What? Is it working?" Jimmy's eyebrows creased and his mouth skewed to one side.

"It's working." said Raj leaning over the phone, "You better come in, Jimmy's having some sort of epiphany in here. Looks like he might crap his pants any minute."

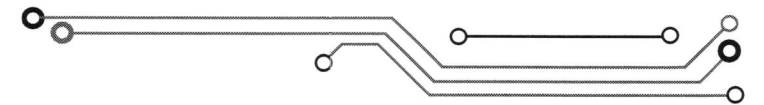

Matt joined them in the office, he had taken the helmet off and all the equipment sat on the desks again. The lines on the dashboard were almost even, grumpy sitting just above happy. "So what's the problem Jimmy?" he asked.

"Well I was suddenly thinking. What is the use of transferring positive energy if there is no net gain? Like if we had to hire someone to sit in a room and think happy thoughts so we can send those thoughts to another room, why not just have the person sit in the other room? Where's the value add?"

The other two looked at each other. It had never occurred to them that there needed to be a value to transferring the energy over a distance. It was just exciting to prove it could be done. Matt had coined a phrase when he first interviewed at Dataffair, "Solving causes". He used it as an example of software developers who have an elegant or interesting bit of code, so they need to create a problem that the code solves. They want to use their idea so bad, they work desperately to find a cause for the problem they have solved. They would invent bizarre use cases that set requirements that needed their solution. He had once seen a developer argue a case where they wanted to reset a user's password if they entered the same wrong password three times in a row. "If they enter the same wrong password three times, that's obviously what they think their password is." he had shouted. The code had already been written, and no matter how many times Matt explained the flaw in the logic to him, the developer just wouldn't get it. They really wanted to use the code they had written to track password entries.

Raj was staring at the helmet. He was solving causes. "What if someone was trapped in a cave, we could send positive energy to them to keep them comfortable during the ordeal." he said out loud, realizing as he said it what he was doing.

"Oh yeah," said Jimmy, "We could have someone walk deep into the cave with a cable, give it to the poor victim, then walk back out, put on the helmet and send positive thoughts their way." He palmed his hand off his own forehead. "C'mon."

"Wait!" said Matt. "That's the problem, we're thinking of sending positive energy to one person. What if we could project positive energy into a room, or an entire building. We don't know how much effect a single positive person can have."

"Wait!" cried Raj now. "What if we had sensors in a ton of different rooms and locations and we routed the positive energy only where it's needed. Instead of cybersecurity, it would be psychic security. We could use the same anomaly detection we use for cyber threats to detect unexpected changes in positivity in companies."

Jimmy's eyes opened wide. "Now we're thinking!" he said. So the question would be, how much positive energy can one person generate and transmit. Even better would be if we could store wells of positive energy that could be tapped into when needed. I guess that's getting ahead of the game though."

"Agreed, I think we need to slow down here," said Matt. "First we need to know if one person can change the energy in an entire room. Then we can worry about negative energy anomaly detection and all those other things." Inside, his brain was spinning like a top. Could it be possible to eliminate negative energy at customers through a centralized positivity factory? That would be a serious disruption to the status quo. Every workplace would be a place of joy. People would actually want to go to work to feel good.

"I want to run some tests tonight before tomorrow's presentation," said Raj. "Let's try the single room idea first. I'm going to record all the data so I can review it tonight and run some tests on it."

Jimmy was already opening the Faraday cage and pulling out the sensor and emitter. He shoved the box under the desk and kicked it. "Ok, this is really the only room we can use. I say we set everything up here. Then I'll stay in the room so it has an organic energy array and Matt can try to change it from out in the main office."

"That makes sense to me." said Raj and leaving his laptop began to walk out of the room.

Matt grabbed the helmet and magic box before leaving. "Don't get too positive." he joked as he left.

"I'll only be grumpy because you're dopey." Jimmy responded

as he shut the door on Matt's back, happy to use his joke. For the rest of the day they tested their device and always got the same results. When Matt was thinking positive thoughts, the "happy" energy in the room went up. When he had sad or negative thoughts, the positive energy in the room was squashed by the grumpy line. By 7:00 p.m. they were tired and agreed to head home and come back tomorrow ready to go. Raj was going to work on getting some statistics out of the data, Matt was going to build their presentation slide deck based on the psychic security idea, and Jimmy was going to paint the helmet and try and make it look more saleable.

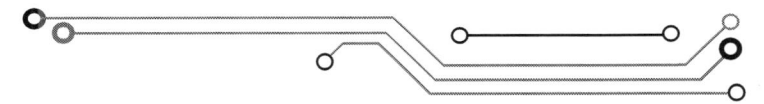

Gillian was talking to Cheryl on the phone when the guys left Cheryl had called to let her know that Bev Shepherd had arrived and checked into her hotel. Apparently she was thrilled to be helping out Gillian, she had made quite an impression on her when they had been on the panel together. Bev wanted to know if she would have time to do a speech before or after the judging. Gillian was thrilled, and she knew the team would be ecstatic. Hearing Bev Shepherd talk usually cost over $50 per person, if you could even get a ticket. "Absolutely!" she cried into the phone. Cheryl filled her in on the details of the final day of hackathon and they hung up.

Malcolm raised his eyebrows from across the table, "What's up?" he asked. Gillian explained about the speech and Malcolm was overjoyed. "I think I've read everything Bev Shepherd ever bothered to speak, write or code. She is an example of a CEO that created a legacy. Did you know that NextGig was her first startup? She was at Nortel before that. I mean, she is a total visionary who saw an entire market before anyone else was even noticing it."

"I did actually," laughed Gillian. "Between you and Matt we may need Cheryl to get extra paper towels to wipe up the drool."

"I'll try to keep it together," said Malcolm, "but I'm not making any promises."

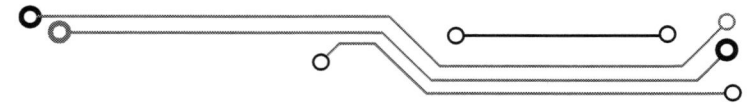

Friday came in like a river dancer on speed. Most of the teams were in by 7:00 a.m. They huddled together in their groups frantically clicking away on keyboards and drawing on whiteboards. Even Mike was early. He had brought in a cardboard cutout of Wayne Gretzky with a speech balloon over his head that said "I'm Wayne Gretzky and I'm turning 7UP". They had a security camera pointed down the aisle of desks and Sachet was waddling the cutout back and forth towards the camera as Nasser and Mike argued about something on their laptops.

Matt, Raj and Jimmy had once again shut themselves up in Mike's office. No one had seen them since they had gone in. Andrea and Daniel were at a whiteboard with hundreds of Internet addresses written on it in neat columns. Another team was on their phones, cables linking them directly to their laptops and high-fiving each other over some secret success. The last team were on the couches head in hands staring at their screens wondering if they would present anything.

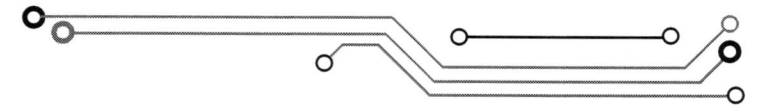

Gillian, Malcolm, and Cheryl were setting up chairs in the kitchen area. They had blown the budget at the wholesale club and bought 25 folding chairs. They had wheeled their office chairs in for the judges. They placed these at the front and then arranged the folding chairs behind them. They had a microphone attached to a podium with an amplifier connected to it. Presentations were due to start just after lunch. Each team would have 30 minutes to present their project, then the judges would meet together and the winners announced at dinner. Gillian had found an old trophy at a thrift shop that had a large silver angel holding a wreath above it's head. Malcolm had taken it to a trophy store and had the old plague peeled off and a new one made. At one point they thought of leaving 'Canadian Interuniversity Sport, Curling Champions 1991' on it as a joke, but decided against it. They had dragged the two picnic tables to one wall and the trophy sat on them along with a buffet of muffins, fruits and danishes.

Malcolm looked around the room with a fixed gaze. He rubbed his hands together, everything was great. He couldn't wait for Bev Shepherd to arrive and he was even more excited to hear her speak. They had decided to put her speech after the presentations. Otherwise they felt she would steal the thunder of the teams. Nolan was already in and on the phone in reception. He was calling members of his sales mafia and getting their feedback on his latest sales adventure. He was apparently also setting up some sales visits for when he got back to California.

Mayor Dickinson didn't have far to travel and his secretary had confirmed that he would be there. Malcolm felt they couldn't be anymore prepared. He hoped the teams would truly impress Ms. Shepherd with their presentations. Sometimes the projects at hackathons got a little out of hand or became jokes instead of a real project, but he believed in his staff.

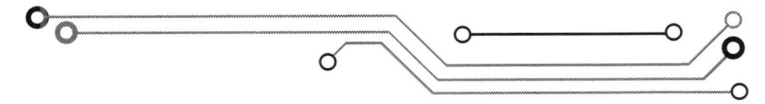

The first team to present was made up of two staff and a co-op student. They had a beautiful slide deck and their speaker was clear and concise. They presented a product similar to Log Driver except for mobile devices. They had named it "Log Roller". Clients would be able to track their corporate phones for malicious activities as easily as their laptop and desktop computers. The rest of the staff applauded and the judges wrote endlessly in their notepads. Each judge then asked questions relevant to their area. Bev Shepherd's questions were very insightful. She showed a full understanding of the effort that had gone into the project, as well as the problems it was trying to solve. The Mayor's questions were more open ended, looking for where this type of project could lead, and how it could help the community. Nolan's questions were all about dollars. Could this be sold per device? Could they add GPS tracking to the app? What was the next upsell for this product?

The second team had attempted to build what was called a honeypot in cybersecurity. It was a computer that was purposely left exposed to lure a hacker into accessing it. It then contained tools to track the hacker and learn about their techniques. Unfortunately while testing it they had lured so many intrusion attempts the machine had quickly been overwhelmed and shut down. Each time they turned it back on it was only minutes before it was terminated again or they lost connection to it as it became too busy to respond to their requests. Originally they were going to name the project Winnie, but in the end it was just Pooh.

Nasser, Mike, and Sachet went third. Mike hefted his body up a step ladder and mounted the team's security camera to the drop ceiling with some zip ties. Nasser was presenting and went to the podium and placed his laptop on it. Sachet stood beside Nasser, his arm around Wayne Gretzky. They had named their project "Face Off". Nasser brought up their slide deck on the big screen and began their presentation. He explained that not only could their cameras now recognize employees' faces, but they were also location aware. Sachet sauntered down in front of the judges, smiling at them as he went. On the screen a display logged "Sachet Singh, enters kitchen 3:10 p.m. Eastern" as he moved passed the camera. When he got past where the camera could recognize him, a new line appeared "Sachet Singh, exits kitchen 3:11 p.m. Eastern". Nasser explained that customers would be able to search by user, location, or time to find out who was in any location at any point. This would allow them to investigate incidents easily.

"We can finally find out who's been eating my lunch," yelled Jimmy from the back. There was a round of chuckles.

Nasser smiled, but continued the demonstration, as Sachet carried Wayne Gretzky in front of him. The system logged "Unknown person 01, enters kitchen 3:15 p.m. Eastern".

"Face Off will automatically tag unknown persons of interest with an ID number, then track that same person throughout the building. This means we can even track Wayne as he moves even if there are other unknown persons wandering about. Each of those people will have their own ID so that we can follow them individually." explained Nasser. "When security gets an alert, they can update this ID to the person's real name and add details including when they are expected to leave. The system won't alert them again until after that time." This caused a round of applause. Nasser noted that Malcolm was nodding his head, and the judges seemed impressed with what his team had accomplished. He went into some of the technical details and problems they had resolved during the course of the contest. Mike stood disinterested by the side chewing on his fingernails during the entire presentation.

Nasser finished off with a slide about where they thought the project should go from here. They would like to add floor plan mappings so they could have dots representing people moving about and alerts on odd congregations of people in one place, or when people who didn't usually interact suddenly did.

Everyone clapped as the presentation ended and the judges huddled together quickly while the next group set up. Malcolm was thinking about the combination of physical and cyber security. It's true you didn't want ne'er-do-wells just wandering into your location and running programs on your computers, or inserting USB sticks with remote access on them, but did it fit with where they were going.

If they started down this path, they may wind up selling security cameras and then having to install them, there was the manufacturing costs and inventory. He really liked the idea, but felt it was a better fit for a company already doing physical security. He was pretty sure the team just wanted to use AI for facial recognition and came up with the idea in order to do that. He smiled to himself remembering Matt always called that "Solving Causes".

He noted Bev Shepherd had finished taking notes on the presentation, he wondered what she was thinking of all this nonsense. Probably believed they should be working on real products instead of wasting almost a week creating throw-away, hobby code. He relaxed a bit in his chair and tried to put on a face that he was both proud of his team and their projects, but also mildly disappointed that they were doing any of this when they had just launched their actual service. At least he hoped that's what Bev Shepherd would see it as.

The fourth team was Andrea and Daniel. Andrea glared at Jimmy as she stood behind the podium. "Our team is called 'Jimmy must die'." she started. "Jimmy as in 'Jimmy a window', obviously not Jimmy the traitor sitting in the audience."

Jimmy looked stunned. "I wasn't even on your team!" he whined.

"No, but you left Sachet, so Sachet stole Nasser. We're all about the root cause on Team Jimmy Must Die." retorted Andrea. She continued without giving him a chance to plead his case.

"We developed a crawler that goes through leaked passwords, encrypts them and then checks if that encrypted value matches any of the encrypted passwords used on a server. If they match, then we know the original password and it means someone is using an old password that has already been leaked." She began to run through their slides on issues they had and how they eventually solved the major problem of checking for leaked passwords without knowing the passwords.

Malcolm thought this idea was excellent. They could easily create a table of the most commonly used passwords and check those as well. It was simple and should be an easy upsell for existing clients in the future. He noted Nolan seemed eager to hear more about this project. Maybe hackathons did work, Malcolm thought, if we have a new product that just needs to be cleaned up and it's ready to go, that would be amazing. He was one of the most enthusiastic in his applause at the end of the presentation.

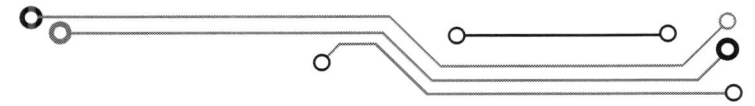

The final presentation was team Psi Phi. Raj went to the podium and connected his laptop for the slides. They planned on doing a live demo for most of the presentation so the slide deck was very short. There were a few slides about how they came up with the helmet, and a few at the end about where they could go from here with Psychic Security. He smiled at everyone as he waited for Matt and Jimmy to get set up. Normally speaking in front of the small familiar group wouldn't be an issue for Raj, but he found the addition of Bev and the Mayor to be causing him a bit of anxiety.

They hadn't brought their extreme cable so Jimmy was running the signal through a network switch to extend the distance from Matt to the sensor. They had placed Matt in the reception area, where everyone could see him, but he was far enough away that it proved the energy was actually travelling through their system. Raj noticed Matt's shirt had "By reading this shirt you agree to my terms and conditions." printed on it in black lettering. He smiled and shook his head. He was ready to begin.

"Everyone knows that engaged employees are more productive, detail oriented and creative." Raj began. "Security is a people problem. A breach is often caused by an overwhelmed employee failing to apply a software patch, or a mistake made in an uninspired moment when they weren't thinking clearly. Many companies have tried different things to keep their employees alert and clear-headed. From exercising first thing in the day to free coffee and nap rooms, it has all been done."

"What most companies miss is that it only takes one negative staff member to sap the energy from the room. When one director is yelling, an entire team can become complacent. When a manager is having a bad day, it can lead to employees being disengaged."

Malcolm was really beginning to wonder where this was going. In the back of his mind he wondered if this was an intervention. He started running through the last month in his head of any talks he had with Raj, Jimmy or Matt.

"We have built this sensor," Raj continued, holding up the end of the network cable with a tiny circuit board attached to it, "to detect the amount of positive and negative energy in the room." Malcolms eyebrows shot up. "This graph I'm displaying now, shows the current values we are picking up in the room. I say the room, but it is picking up mostly my energy right now since I'm holding it, it would be better in the ceiling or mounted somewhere central." Raj watched the grumpy line begin to creep up. He decided to own it. "The negative line you see creeping up is because I'm super nervous right now." The team laughed, which made Raj laugh and they watched the line sink again. This brought a round of applause from everyone which sent the positive line even higher.

Malcolm had one eye squinting, even as he clapped with the others. How was this related at all to what Dataffair was doing. He really hoped this didn't embarrass the company in front of Ms. Shepherd. He glanced over at her applauding, she was smiling. He didn't know if it was because she thought it was a joke, or was actually liking the presentation.

"So you can see that the sensor is picking up on the positive vibes in the room," Raj said, feeling better now. "We discovered in our testing that there is a finite amount of energy in a space. If negative energy goes up, then positive energy must go down. A room full of positive energy creates positive employees, better interactions between them and keeps them motivated and at the top of their game. However, all it takes is one negative staffer to enter the room and that energy can be completely sapped."

Jimmy was on the side of the makeshift stage. He started pinching himself and working up a good head of steam. He thought about that kid that had blown up his enormous cathedral on his Minecraft server. He'd spent years building it and then one kid who 'just wanted to see it' blew the whole thing up. He had restored it from a backup, but it just didn't feel the same, it had lost something. He was good and angry as he stormed out beside Raj. Immediately the negative line shot up and the positive went to zero. Raj continued

"You can see my friend Angry Jim here just blew out all the positive energy we had created, if this was a company and Jimmy stayed upset, the entire office would be affected. We'd all start having negativity in our thoughts and then the positive energy would never recover. Luckily team Psi Phi has created a product that solves this problem, we can detect and remediate negative energy spikes as they happen and keep the entire office working like a dream."

Malcolm could feel his jaw slip away from the rest of his face. He was beginning to see where this was going and he felt incredibly embarrassed, not just for himself, but for everyone in the room.

"We're calling it the Psi-Phone!" Raj ad libbed. Jimmy looked at him with a puzzled expression and then suddenly smiled. Raj thought it was pretty good too. Matt was giving the thumbs up from the reception area. Malcolm was smiling, but only with his mouth, his eyes were burning coals behind his glasses. He pushed the rims hard into his nose before clapping with everyone else.

"Matt is about to send positive energy into the room." Raj looked at the graph. "Oh, and apparently Jimmy is going to have to bring us back to negativity somehow." Jimmy had lost focus with the surprise name announcement and had forgotten all about his beloved citadel in Minecraft. He tried thinking of it again but couldn't bring it to mind. He went deeper and thought about high school and the negativity began to flow. What a waste of time it was! You learned nothing important during high school except not to trust people. The negative line quickly shot back up to full.

Matt saw Raj give him the thumbs up. He returned the symbol and cleared his mind. He began thinking of winning the hackathon. Maybe getting a paper published on their work in a medical journal or business magazine. He wrapped his hands together thinking of the notoriety this would bring. Matt Reynolds, famous inventor, who had changed the world, bringing people together in extreme joy and bliss.

At the podium, Raj was beginning to feel the awkward silence. The lines weren't changing. He could feel the stares of everyone watching and waiting. Why wasn't it working? He looked from Jimmy to Matt. The difference between the two was drastic. Jimmy's face was a ball of anger as he focused on some brutal thought. Matt's face was blissful, his eyes closed as he dreamed of something wonderful.

Meanwhile, Raj was becoming a sweaty mess of anxiety. He checked the sensor and emitter, it seemed fine, everything secure and connected. His eyes followed the cord back towards Matt. Someone coughed, shattering the silence and making Raj feel even more anxious. His eyes reached the network switch they had used to cobble the cables together and went wide. Instantly he realized the problem. A network switch was designed to pass on network signals only. It would be ignoring the positive energy signals assuming they were noise on the line and only passing on actual packets. This wasn't going to work with a switch in the line.

"One second folks," he stuttered into the microphone, "there's a kink in the cable." He put the sensor on the podium and ran to Mike's office, all eyes watching as he tore out of the room. He grabbed their box of network cable and rushed back in. He could feel the tension in the room as he quickly swapped the cable in the sensor and then ran the other end to the reception room. The silence was almost unbearable. As he pushed the connector into the magic box it was the loudest, most satisfying click he had ever heard. Then he heard the intake of breath from everyone in the kitchen area. He rushed back to look at the screen. Happy had streaked back to the top pushing grumpy down to almost nothing. He could see Jimmy begin to lose his anger, unable to fight against the wave of energy flowing from the emitter.

"Sorry about that," Raj said breathlessly. "We had a network switch in the line and it saw our signal as just noise. It was properly filtering it out." He placed both hands on the podium and breathed. He could feel the energy as well, he started to feel good about how things were going. When he looked out now all he saw was friends. He was beginning to realize the power of what they had built. His anxiety flowed from him with every exhale. This truly worked and he was an unwitting test subject. He almost started to laugh. He felt giddy as he glanced at Jimmy who was now smiling, his eyes encouraging Raj to continue.

"Can everyone feel the positivity?" he asked. There were nods and hands raised. As he scanned the room he saw all 3 judges smiling and nodding their heads. It made sense as they were the closest to the emitter. "We could train Positivity Technicians, or Positechs as we would call them, to emit pure bliss signals through mantras and meditation. We can easily monitor our clients negative energy and when there are spikes, direct our positive energy to that client. A short term burst of positivity will immediately rectify the issue, and then the positivity maintains itself through the subjects in the room. Matt no longer has to focus and send positive energy our way because everyone here is now exuding positivity." Raj was beaming as he spoke. The group was all smiling as well. He realized it may be the positive energy they were emitting into the room, but he was ok with that. Even Cheryl standing at the back was smiling and nodding her head. Oddly, the only one that didn't look excited was Malcolm. He had this weird look on his face. Raj couldn't really place it. It was like he just realized his cat had eaten his favourite pet goldfish.

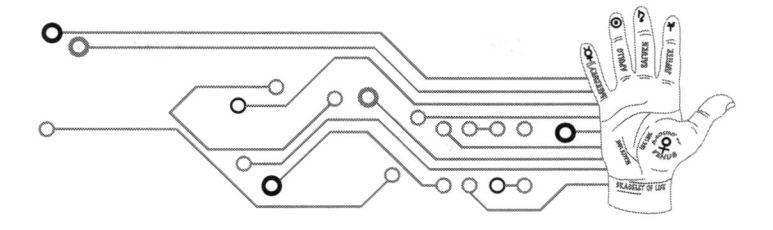

CHAPTER 0000 0111: JUDGEMENT DAY

Everyone was mingling waiting for the judges to deliberate, so Bev could make her speech and they could head out to dinner. Malcolm was leaning against the kitchen counter, one hand on the counter, the other bringing a glass of Scotch to his mouth. Gillian had never seen him actually drink the Scotch before and was stunned he was on his second glass. "Well that was something," he said, taking the glass away from his mouth. "A lot of interesting projects."

"Definitely." Gillian responded. "I'm amazed at what people can come up with when you just let them create. The positive energy thing was unbelievable. Who would've thought of that?"

"Yeah. Who?" Malcolm said despondent. "That was a joke right? I mean 'Positive energy' travelling over the network keeping everyone motivated. It's not very believable."

"You saw the graphs." Gillian commented, opening the fridge beside her and grabbing a can of vodka soda. "It appeared to be working, and I certainly felt more motivated." She popped the top of the can, then turned the tab sideways. She had picked that up in university, marking a drink as hers and making it easier to track.

"Yeah, but that could have all been smoke and mirrors." replied Malcolm staring into his own glass. "I mean, I get that being excited gets others excited. Just them jumping around and getting all worked up would affect everyone in the room. It doesn't mean they transferred the energy across a network cable, right?" He looked up at her. She could see he wanted it to be a rhetorical question, but that he wasn't sure if it was.

"I believed it," she said frankly. "I'm kind of fascinated by the implications of it. It has some ethical questions that go along with it too."

"Alright, well what about the others," Malcolm slid into a topic change. "Which one could we actually productize?" His face returned to the normal Malcolm. Back to business.

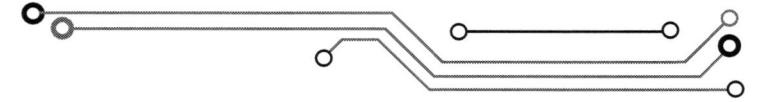

The judges were sitting in Mike's office, the door was closed and they had notepads resting on their laps. Mayor John Dickinson had his legs crossed in their gray slacks. He was balding on top and his white hair hung straight down from the fringe around the back half of his head. He had on large glasses and a golf shirt from a local golf club. The shirt was hunter green with an almost glowing coyote paw print embroidered into it. This was the club's logo, but it was also one of the Mayor's problems, the number of coyotes in the green spaces that Waterloo was known for. He had a warm smile as he talked, and his smooth voice had just enough of a British accent to sound elegant. He had previously been a minister and you could imagine a congregation soaking in his sermons. As Bev looked at him while he spoke she was picturing his voice as the next virtual assistant, but she wouldn't call it John, she was thinking Nigel.

"I'm impressed with the innovation in all of these projects," he was saying. "I didn't understand a lot of the technical information and requirements they mentioned, but they certainly made it easy to understand what the end result would be. It's exactly what this city is known for Bev." He turned his attention directly to her, "Waterloo would be the perfect place for a NextGig location. The talent pool is second to none and I could certainly help finding a location."

Bev smiled looking at the mayor, "NextGig is doing ok in Ottawa, but thanks." She put her pen on the pad and rested her arms on the rests of her chair. She was wearing a stylish red leather jacket with a black blouse underneath. She had black jeans on with high boots that almost reached her knee. "I'm not actually that involved in NextGig these days, Marissa Morgan has taken over as CEO, but I will certainly let her know that you are interested and give her your card." John immediately dove into his pocket and pulled out an entire deck of business cards. "That'd be great!" he exclaimed as he dealt a card to both Bev and Nolan.

"As for the hackathon projects, I have to say, I'm equally as impressed as John. For such small teams they truly did amazing things. I enjoy these types of events, they get people thinking in new directions, there are no limitations on their thoughts. I feel like it's a freedom a lot of developers don't get in their normal work days." She picked up her pad of paper and flipped to the last page. "I have to go make a short talk, so I'm going to just get down to it, this is my list for technical prowess and meaningfulness ... or what did they call it? Solid melons?"

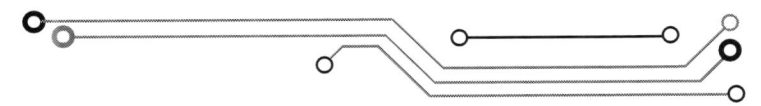

Cheryl walked to the podium and banged on it with her palm. She shook her hair out of her face. She was extremely happy that everyone would soon board the limo bus to the restaurant and she would be done organizing for the week. She had already booked Monday off to relax. "If everyone could take their seats please." she announced. Most of the team started to move right away. Malcolm rushed, without appearing to rush, to get to a front seat. He noted that Matt was already there. He quickly excused himself as he squeezed past slow movers. Nasser and Jimmy were standing by the kegerator. They kept it beside the fridge and were very proud of their two taps and the craft beers they poured. They purchased it directly from a brewery in Ayr, a small town just outside the region. The kegerator for Dataffair was like the water cooler of old. Ideas were shared, problems solved and gossip on the latest in tech and pop culture was aired. Both Jimmy and Nasser had full glasses and were obviously in a heated debate when the announcement was made. As everyone sat down they could hear Jimmy loudly arguing "Cake can have filling. There are lots of cakes with fillings."

"You can't count icing a cake and then placing another cake on top as 'filling'," Nasser exclaimed, making air quotes. He was staring directly into Jimmy's eyes, which were looking directly back at him.

Cheryl leaned in way too close to the microphone and shouted out "Naaaaaassssserrrr and Jimmmmmmeeee," in a husky voice. Jimmy's head spun around so quickly his hood flew over his shoulder, the pull strings going around the back. Nasser jumped enough that his beer sloshed over the side of his glass. He held it up as the foam dripped down the side. Cursing as he began to walk to the chairs and take a seat, attempting to catch the drips in his other hand. "The cake is a lie!" he shouted to no one in particular.

"Dataffair has a very special presentation today from one of the top executives in Canada." Cheryl ignored Nasser's outburst.

"Gillian is going to introduce her, thanks Gillian." There was a round of applause as Gillian got up and went to the front.

"I first met our guest in Calgary, we were both on a panel for Code Like A Girl, a social enterprise providing the tools and confidence for women to enter the technology workspace. I was impressed by her self-confidence, drive and understanding of the software business. She has been an executive at Nortel and launched her own company, NextGig, when she realized there was a new wave of up and coming technologies that she wanted to be a part of. I hope you will all give a warm welcome to someone that I like to call a mentor and a friend, Bev Shepherd!" Gillian stepped back and clapped with the rest of the group as Bev strode to the front. Bev exuded confidence just in the way she walked. There was no question that this was a woman who would tell you how she felt, yet her smile and eyes told a different story. Someone who would listen to, and consider opposing views as well. Gillian smiled, she had a feeling of pride about being associated with such a role-model, and she was excited to hear what Bev would say.

Malcolm was clapping enthusiastically. This was the portrait he wanted to portray to his team. As they grew, he knew he wouldn't know everyone personally. You had to make a clear impression on the staff that you knew what you were doing without talking to them individually. Bev was doing that. Everything about her reinforced that you could trust her, she was smart, capable and would have your back in any situation.

Bev adjusted the microphone to her height and shook her hair back before beginning. "Good afternoon Dataffair!" she said loudly and received a roaring response of whistles and shouts.

"I've been to a lot of hackathon presentations, as well as pitches for investments, and generally people trying to sell me their ideas.

This group did an amazing job of presenting their projects and I'm blown away at how much you have all accomplished in just days. Congratulations to everyone here. I, myself, don't know the results yet, but I've handed in my votes and I'm excited to see the final results." She paused and placed her hands on the edges of the lectern.

"Once NextGig went to initial public offering, I found myself the subject of many interviews. In the beginning, the media wanted to focus on a woman launching a public technology company. I don't control the media," she smiled and added "yet." which made the group laugh. "But I was disappointed in them, I felt like they were focusing on the wrong thing. We were launching a social change from a 9 to 5 job to a time when you did many jobs, things you enjoyed and were paid for your talent, not your time. I truly felt this should be the focus of what the press was talking about."

"Over time though I realized that I was something new, even though I didn't feel it. I've always been me as far back as I can remember." As the group laughed again, everyone's eyes were wide, they were waiting on her next word. The power of her voice and tone drew them in as if mesmerized. "It was ok that they needed to ask questions about something they'd never seen before. To many I was like an alien that just showed up and wanted to talk about climate change. The media was focused on the 'Holy crap it's an alien!' part and were missing the message. I just needed to keep my focus and answer their questions and help them learn that a woman in technology wasn't the story. I was only new for a while, other 'aliens' landed as well, it was becoming 'common' and eventually that same media stopped asking about my feelings and gender and began asking where I saw jobs and the economy in the future. They started asking how I led a team of ten to become a team of ten thousand with over five billion dollars in revenue. To steal a term from a real estate friend, they finally saw past the paint colour."

"As your company grows, people aren't always going to see your dream right away. They don't know what your goals are, and they may not even see the direction you are going. You can't let this bring you down or cause you to change your ideas. You need to stay consistent and wait for them to see the change you are creating. Whatever you are doing, you need to educate, not dictate." She paused here and looked out at the gathering. She smiled as her glance passed Gillian who was nodding her head.

"I always start my talk that way, since it's a message that needs to be reinforced, but today I'd like to talk to you about the things that did change me as I grew NextGig, you see the media isn't the only one that needs a message reinforced to grow, we all do. I was the same way. When I started NextGig the point was to disrupt the status quo, and I've been called a disrupter," she then added out of the side of her mouth, "as well as many other things." She beamed as she waited for the chuckles to end. "NextGig was, and still is, changing the economy on a global scale. What I learned is that 'Think global, act local' applies to more than just reusable coffee cups." Bev shifted her weight to one foot and lifted her hands.

"I was helping people find jobs and live a better life in Ashland, Nebraska, but forgetting about the jobs, and the lifestyles of my own staff. People are what make a company work. Without the team I had at the beginning, NextGig wouldn't be here today. Sure, they say 'No one is irreplaceable' and I believe it. I myself have been replaced as CEO now. But the fact that someone can be replaced doesn't make them replaceable." She paused here, to let it sink in.

"I have an example I use with developers a lot. All of your hackathon code is on your laptops right now, how many of you have a backup of that code stored remotely somewhere." Every hand shot up. Bev laughed and threw up her hands "Surprise." she said sarcastically and the group laughed. "So I want to ask a few of you, would you care if I stole your laptop? It can easily be replaced, heck, it may even be an upgrade for some of you based on the number of stickers I see plastered on your cases. I'll start with the beer spiller," she pointed out Nasser, who made a face at being known as the beer spiller. "You seem like a relaxed guy. How hard would it be to replace your laptop?"

Nasser stood, even though he wasn't sure he was supposed to. He muttered a bit and then replied "Well, I wouldn't want to do it. I don't actually back up my configuration. And I have a lot of scripts that run on login that I'd have to recreate. Frankly, it would suck." He took his seat again.

Bev looked over the crowd. "Now, if you were this gentleman, what would you do to solve his issue?"

"Back up your configs!" shouted Jimmy without waiting.

"Exactly!" exclaimed Bev, pointing at Jimmy. "You would create backups of everything that made your laptop unique. You want to be able to take a blank, off-the-shelf machine, and create a clone of what you had. This is what developers do!" She exclaimed. "We want things to be repeatable .... duplicated ... run in parallel ... the exact ... same ... every ... time." She paused for effect.

"You see, this is fine for machines, like our laptops, but we need to realize people are different."

"We start creating coding style rules, processes, standards and then we begin applying them to people. We want to make it so if Bob leaves the company, Alice can step in right behind and replace him as an exact duplicate. We remove the personality. Right now, this man's laptop has eyebrows, as Frank Zappa would say. It has a personality to it that makes it unique and different from every other laptop here." She pointed over the crowd. "Even his Hello Kitty sticker makes it so that he can recognize it." The group laughed again. "It may not be the best laptop in the world, but it is his. Now I'm not saying having different and unique laptops is a great business, but it is for people. That's something it took me a while to learn."

"Opportunities like this hackathon allow people to express themselves. It allows them to own something they thought of and crafted themselves. This is what keeps employees engaged and motivated and will serve you much better than processes and standards ever will."

"A lot of you may already know that before I left NextGig I changed the name of the Human Resources team to Human Relations. You could say that is the demarcation point where I finally learned that a company wasn't just the processes and ideas I had put in place, but it was made up of unique individuals that gave NextGig a personality. This wasn't just the upper management like Marissa Morgan that eventually took over, but the developers, project managers, catering staff and security guards. They all affected how NextGig operated and how successful we were."

"As a startup it's easy to remember how important every staff member is. And just like this gentlemans laptop, everyone is unique and brings different things to the table. As you grow, your IT team will begin to create processes to provision laptops and configure them exactly the same. They will track the work done on that machine remotely, they will 'backup your configs' as was said. It's the way companies grow, we standardize things and create processes to ensure the status quo across the corporation. The trick, and the point of my talk today, is to not let that happen to your people."

"I have a final story that I think drives this point home." Bev paused to look at the small team. She had them all she noticed, the various beverages were held in their laps, eyes were on her, she felt like she was a preacher, standing at the lectern talking to her flock.

"We originally contracted our kitchen staff when NextGig grew big enough to sustain a true cafeteria. One of the chef's from this contract crew noticed the increasing popularity of shawarma." There was an audible murmur among the gathered team. "Yes," Bev laughed, "it has become the fuel of the tech industry. This chef, on their own time created a new shawarma sauce and called it NextGigGarlic. They made it exclusively for the NextGig staff. Has anyone here had the chance to try it?"

Matt and Gillian raised their hands. Malcolm turned and stared at Matt with a surprised look on his face. "I interviewed there before I started here." Matt explained, shrugging. "That shawarma is amazing."

"It is!" said Bev, "And not only was it great tasting, it raised productivity 5%. The management team spent a lot of time analyzing data attempting to figure out why we were suddenly beating deadlines and surpassing sales figures. In the style of Freakonomics we eventually traced it back to the joy that the shawarma created in the staff. Good food was causing good vibes. People were more engaged and happy to be at work. Our remote staff began to drop into the office more often. It wasn't that people were staying in the office for lunch and spending more time working. In fact, we verified that lunch breaks had actually got extended due to more staff chatting together in the cafeteria. They weren't always talking about work, but they were enjoying themselves. This motivated them to become a better team, they supported each other more.

Our kudos program started getting used 25% more during the initial launch of NextGigGarlic. Now as a side note, afternoons in our nap room also became a scheduling nightmare." Bev laughed and everyone laughed with her.

"NextGig created the NextGigGourmet company and hired all of the cafeteria contract staff. They had complete autonomy and created and managed what they served. This was a great example of how having the ability to make decisions and be part of the company instead of working for the company made all the difference. We use that in our job descriptions now, we are looking for people who want to be part of the wave, not surf on top of it."

"I want to end with a huge congratulations again to all teams, the projects you presented were astounding! Keep creating and keep dreaming. Thank you." She smiled as the gathering stood and applauded. She bowed slightly and backed away from the lectern and returned to her seat. The applause lasted long after she had sat down.

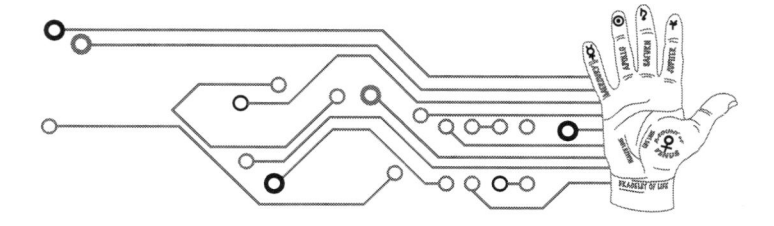

CHAPTER 0000 1000: THE RESULTS ARE IN

The crew stormed off the limo bus and into the Code and Clam. They had reserved a private room and the hostess was quick to usher the boisterous group through the other diners and into the back. Cheryl didn't follow, she instead went straight to the bar for a large glass of Pinot Grigio. When she finally entered the room she had the glass in one hand and the rest of the bottle in the other. The restaurant had laid out a single large rectangular table. Malcolm and Gillian sat at one end with the three judges flanking them. The rest of the staff filled in the seats, with Cheryl and Jimmy taking the foot of the table. There were already toasted bread rolls and platters of nachos, overflowing with toppings on the table. Flasks of wine and pitchers of beer were placed between every few people and glasses were quickly filled as everyone tucked themselves in for a feast.

In the middle of the table resting on a raised platform, surrounded by flowers, sat the goal of the evening, the hackathon trophy for best project. Above this were hung a giant inflatable hammer and screwdriver made by their business neighbour. There was a large banner strung between them that said "Dataffair:

Building Great Things".

The chatter started almost immediately and Malcolm and Gillian decided to let everyone have a chance to converse before any formal announcements to kick things off. The Mayor appeared to be chewing Bev's ear off and Malcolm decided he would have to separate them at some point. Nolan was getting details from Raj about what customer size Dataffair could handle. Gillian had gone down the table and was talking to Andrea and Daniel. Malcolm was impressed at how easily she could join a conversation. He always wound up like this, waiting for someone to come to him. It wasn't that he couldn't talk about different things, but he always felt if he started the conversation it wouldn't be something the other person was interested in. His interests tended to be things others wanted to avoid. He also assumed this is what made him great management material.

He looked at the makeshift hackathon trophy sitting in the middle of the table. In a way he felt that it was just like him. It didn't really fit here, it wasn't supposed to be a hackathon trophy, it was a curling trophy. It was still a thing of beauty, the angel shone in the restaurant lights and held the wreath over its head with dignity. That trophy was doing its best impression of a hackathon trophy, even though it wasn't sure what that was. He was doing his best impression of a social, fun-loving entrepreneur, even though he didn't really know what that felt like.

Matt slid into Gillian's chair beside him, placing an oversized glass of beer on the table. "I think that went off brilliantly." he said looking into Malcolm's glasses. "You know," he suddenly interrupted his own conversation, "if you switched to round frames, you could pull off a pretty good Harry Potter."

"Thanks!" said Malcolm with a hint of sarcasm. "Office

Halloween costume all sorted." He leaned forward and cupped his glass of Scotch with both hands and stared into it. "Your project was a bit out of left field."

"Right?" said Matt with excitement. "If you had asked me last week, the idea of positive energy, let alone the transfer of it, would have been the last thing on my mind. I can tell you, when we were testing it, you could really feel it. Oddly, I can't really describe what it felt like. It wasn't like you were overwhelmed with bubbly happiness, you just felt … safer, if that makes any sense."

Malcolm wasn't sure that it did make sense. "So you believe it was actually working and it wasn't that you've figured out how to transfer some white noise from one point to another?"

Matt made an inquisitive look, "I never thought about that. I guess it's possible we were just sending noise … but it doesn't explain how it made us feel. Heck, even Jimmy seemed more content."

Malcolm looked at him, not sure what to think. "Well, it was definitely the most creative project I've seen come out of a hackathon," he said and Matt felt that the word 'creative' was being used as a four letter word. Gillian interrupted their talk from the other end of the table.

"OK everyone back to your seats, we're going to take care of business and announce the winners and then get our party on." Cheryl handed her four envelopes as she walked back to the head of the table. Malcolm stood up to join her, pushing his glasses back as she handed him two of the envelopes.

"We're going to announce the category winners first and then the total points winner. They are the ones that will have their names engraved on this magnificent trophy you see displayed here." Gillian did her best game show hostess impression pointing out the silver angel in the middle of the table. "Malcolm, would you like to start?"

"Thanks Gillian." Malcolm looked at the front of his first envelope. "Best Presentation" was scrawled out in Cheryl's flowing handwriting. "Our first category award is for the best presentation. This was judged by our Mayor John Dickinson, thank you John. I'm sure this wasn't an easy category to rank."

"No it wasn't!" returned the Mayor, "Congratulations to everyone on your presentations, you made it very difficult to pick only one. You are all winners to me."

Malcolm wondered if the majority of being a politician was keeping a series of platitudes filed away in your memory to pull out whenever you got the chance. He tore the end off the envelope and shook the paper out. "I have the rankings in my hand. And the winner is ...". he looked down at the paper, "Face Off! For their security camera facial recognition software.". There was a round of applause. Nasser and Sachet stood up and began bowing left and right. Mike was clapping Malcolm noted, he wondered if he knew what he was clapping about or if the applause had woke him up.

"Next up," started Gillian, "is the award for the Is it Ripe category. This was judged by our own VP of sales, Nolan Walker." Nolan stood and played to the crowd as Gillian slit the fold of the envelope with her fingernail. She waited for him to sit again before continuing. "And the winner is ... Jimmy Must Die! For their breached password detection project." There was another round of applause.

"Final category winner is for the Not Hollow category judged by our esteemed guest Beverly Shepherd." announced Malcolm clapping enthusiastically as he tore open the envelope. He looked down at the paper and raised his eyebrows in surprise. "And the winner is ... Team Psi Phi for their psi-phone." Jimmy and Matt let out a hoot and high fived at the other end of the table. Raj kept it more casual and appeared to be imitating the Queen with his wave.

"Thanks to everyone for participating!" exclaimed Gillian. "That leaves only the grand winner to be announced. This is a sum of your points across all three categories. This is bragging rights for an entire year and your names permanently engraved in history by the lowest priced artisan we can find." The table eagerly watched as she tore the envelope open and unfolded the sheet inside. "And the winner is ..." she paused, looking around at the faces of her team. "Jimmy Must Die!" she declared to shouts and hollers and a very loud "Boo" from Jimmy as he flopped back in his chair. Andrea and Daniel high-fived each other, then gave a smug look at Nasser and Jimmy.

Shortly after the announcements, dinner was laid out. Discussion was rampant between mouthfuls, and laughter was often heard around the table. Gillian looked around smiling, amazed that an event that just happened already had people reminiscing nostalgically about it. Matt was wearing their psi-phone while he ate and nearby staff were commenting on the various parts, asking questions about the build. It wasn't long before a stack of empty plates was all that was left of dinner. Half trays of soggy nachos were still being picked at and everyone was more relaxed in their chairs, discussing everything from the hackathon to hockey.

The Mayor left as soon as he ate, excusing himself to attend another function. Bev looked like she was holding court at one end of the table with a gathering around her listening to stories of the beginnings of NextGig. Mike was trying to convince Sachet to take one of the signature Code and Clam pint glasses. They were unique in that they were hexagonal and etched with the Code and Clam logo. The logo was a pair of curly braces turned sideways with a semicolon above them. It was supposed to look like a winking clam apparently. But Malcolm always thought they made it so it was the easiest to text when deciding where to go for lunch. ";{}?" was quick and easy. Malcolm and Gillian wound up at the head of the table alone discussing the upcoming sales meeting.

Raj slid into a chair on the corner adjacent to Gillian. He had a bottle of water with him and looked like he just finished getting ready for the night. "Hey guys."

"Hey!" shouted Gillian, her wine was starting to get to her head.

"Hey Raj," said Malcolm, spinning his Scotch glass with his finger tips. "That was an interesting project you came up with. I didn't realize you were so spiritual."

"I'm not sure I would define it as spiritual," replied Raj, "but I have a theory. Interested in hearing it?"

"For sure!" said Gillian, "I find the idea of positive energy transfer fascinating."

Raj dug out his wallet and produced his last student ID card. "Who is this?" he asked, showing them the card.

"That's you." said Malcolm.

"Right!" said Raj. "But it's not. It's a digital reproduction of my image."

"Sure." shrugged Gillian. "It's a picture of you then."

"Exactly. Except it's not that either. It's only made up of dots. If you look really close you can see the dots. Your brain fills in the rest, just makes it up."

"Sure, that's true of a lot of things." said Malcolm, "I'm not sure how this relates to positive energy ..."

"Hang on, it's coming." continued Raj. "So this image was actually taken by a digital camera. The camera just used sensors to detect light, it had no idea that it was taking a picture, it just detected light and wrote a bunch of ones and zeros to a chip. The camera doesn't even know what a picture is, it just wrote the data it knew to the drive. Then that data was transferred from the camera to a computer. The computer didn't know it was a picture either, and it could be argued it wasn't a picture at all, it's just a bunch of data."

"I'm following ..." said Gillian. She was now actually interested in where this was leading.

"So a program on the computer, strips the colour information out of that data, then uses an algorithm to compress all the information. The only reason it can do this is because some computer programmer, who does know what a picture is, told it that if it modified the data this way, people could still recognize the image. The computer then sends the completely new set of ones and zeros to a printer which just plots dots when it reads a one and doesn't when it reads a zero. And after all that, we have this picture. At no time in the process, from me standing there to get the picture taken until you looked at it just now, was it ever a photo. The entire time it was just data."

"Right." said Malcolm. "Computers don't understand that it's a picture, everything is data to them. Long way to get there buddy." he laughed.

"Yeah, yeah." Raj waved it off. "I've been in school for a long time. Anyway, your eyes are the same. They don't know it's a picture of me. They just send along the data and your brain constructs it into my image. It makes up the bits that aren't there.

"I think we're doing the same thing with positive energy, with just one more layer of abstraction. With the energy, we don't even know what we're sending. We're more like the computer in the previous example. We're getting data, we're sending it along, but we don't know what it is. Maybe we're not sending all of it. Maybe we're only sending a few dots of the total picture, but whatever it is we're sending, your brain is making up for it and it's saying "That's positive energy, I recognize it."

"That's my theory. I think that's why Mike can't digitize it, it's because we don't even have the whole picture but we were lucky enough to get just enough that our brains recognize it."

"That's amazing!" said Gillian. "I love that idea. It's so true, we give computers credit for all this facial recognition, but really it should be called data recognition, it doesn't actually understand what a face is even."

"Exactly!" said Raj. "Just like we don't understand what positive energy is exactly, we just know if we send this signal from here to there, our brains interpret that as positivity. If we pictured our signal as an email, we may only be sending half the letters, or just the attachments, or maybe we are sending the whole thing, we don't even know. But we do know we're sending enough that our brains can figure it out."

"Interesting." muttered Malcolm with a far off gaze. "So is it possible that some people's brains wouldn't recognize these pieces of positive energy? Like pattern recognition, the more times you see a pattern the easier you can pick it out."

"So someone that hasn't experienced lots of positivity won't be able to recognize the signal Raj made?" Gillian asked.

"Exactly." Malcolm confirmed, picking up his glass and draining the last of it.

"That would be sad," said Raj. "I guess that's possible. If you've never seen me and I asked you who the picture was, you wouldn't know either. But who hasn't had positivity in their life?"

Malcolm decided to change the subject. "Great theory Raj, but what made you get into all this positivity?"

"Well," began Raj, "when I was in school, I found life pretty easy. I knew what I had to focus on — academics. I was surprised once I started a 'real job' that I found myself ... shiftless I guess. I wind up working all the time because I'm not sure what else to do. Eventually I gave myself three overall goals to take care of, mind, body and soul. So that's when I joined the gym which took care of the body part. I just treat it like an early morning class. Have to get there, do the work and in the end I'll stay in shape. Simple."

"Life is simple, it's just not easy," said Malcolm. "It's fantastic that you are able to do that."

"Thanks," said Raj. "So then it became mind and soul. I still study a lot and the work here has been challenging, so taking care of my mind was the easiest one for me. I love learning and pushing myself to think differently, I'm always looking for new ideas."

"It was the soul part that was being ignored. I didn't come from a religious family, so I was looking for alternatives to an organized group. I wanted something that was spiritual as you called it, but private, internal, something that was about my soul, not every soul on the planet. I was looking at mindfulness which is so popular right now and started meditating. Then I found this old book on the science of higher sense perception. I was kind of fascinated by it. I don't think I believed in E.S.P. or anything like that, but I took the advice in the book, which was basically mantras and programming your subconscious to be more accepting of a higher purpose or state of being. I basically took that advice with my own grain of salt, maybe added a little pepper, did some more research online and started a 'program' of soulful well-being for myself."

"That's fascinating." said Gillian, staring at Raj. "A personal religion of positivity is what you wound up with?"

"Exactly. I mean, I'm still not a hugger. It totally wrinkles your clothes. I just try to keep a positive attitude and an open mind to the wonders around me. Take in joy and bliss and project the same."

Malcolm looked from Gillian to Raj and back again. "But you know that it means nothing right? I mean, if you don't have a higher being in your personal religion, then when you die it doesn't matter how well you lived your life right? Isn't the afterlife the important part of all this religious stuff?"

"I see what you're saying." said Raj, taking some time to phrase his response. "In my personal religion, if that's what we want to call it, it's about what you do in life, while you are living that life, that's important. You reap the benefits immediately, when you die I think you are just gone, your energy joins the rest in the universe and recirculates. For me it's what I do in life that brings joy for me and others. Like you said, life is simple, it's just not easy. Being happy is simple, enjoy what you have and what's around you. But it's not easy, accepting that life is good enough when you don't have that new car or bigger house is the tricky part. Everyone has and wants different things. I may want a spouse, but somewhere there's a guy with a great wife who's longing for a University Degree."

"Is there?" questioned Malcolm, eyebrow raised.

"Like I said, everyone wants different things. What I've found from meditation is the ability to focus on feeling blessed about what I have and less focused on what I don't have. It's worked for me. And then the higher sense perception is just fascinating. When you take out some of the crazy, a lot of it is just about feeling good and positive energy." As he finished he looked sideways. "Anyway, that's where Matt and I came up with the whole project, who doesn't want to be happy?"

"Ha." laughed Malcolm sarcastically, "But no one wants to be crazy and happy."

"Don't they?" retorted Raj. "What do you think, Gillian?"

"I can tell you that in my short 30 something years on this planet, I've dated beer league hockey players that were happy and NHL players that weren't. I think part of it is, you need to keep dreaming. If you don't have a dream, you're not happy with whatever you have. And people that achieve their dream, but then don't create a new one to strive for wind up sad." She took a sip of her wine and then said "And you guys are a total buzz kill, I'm going to talk to Nasser, he looks pissed out of his gourd." She laughed as she got up and walked past Raj roughing his hair up as she passed.

"OH MY GAWD!" he bawled. "I need to go fix this." he sighed as he stood, leaving Malcolm smiling with a distant look on his face as he swirled his Scotch. His eyes widened as he looked down the table and saw Sachet take an empty glass and slide it into his backpack.

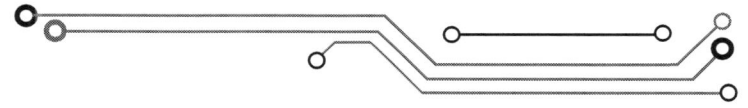

By midnight the team was staggering, waddling and even crawling to the limo bus for their rides home. Bev Shepherd had long ago left for a flight to Colorado. Nasser was singing a song he had apparently learned as a child at camp, but no one could figure out what language it was in. Jimmy had his hoodie up and the ties pulled so tight you could barely make out his face. He had stolen the inflatable hammer from the display and was running around the outside of the group hitting them over the head with it. Then he would shout or sometimes whisper in their ear, "You're hammered!"

Matt couldn't wait to get home, his wife and kids would be arriving sometime tomorrow afternoon and he had big plans to greet them. Gillian was planning to walk to her local pub as soon as she was dropped off to meet up with friends. Sachet was clinking along, his backpack over his shoulder, telling anyone who would listen "I don't usually do things like this." Mike would laugh every time. Raj was telling Malcolm that he was going to research aura generation this weekend. He wondered if you could detect aura's by creating a new type of camera.

Malcolm was going home. He would work on the sales slide deck and maybe give his parents a call this weekend.

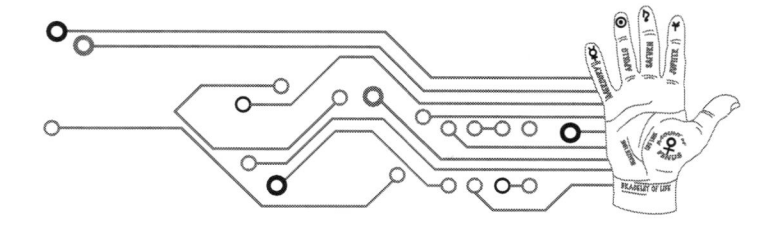

CHAPTER 0000 1001:
THE SALES MAFIA MAKES A HIT

The law firm of Heller & Associates was in downtown Kitchener. You couldn't really tell when you crossed from uptown Waterloo to downtown Kitchener, but the longer you lived in the city, the more you were aware of when you had migrated from one to the other. Gillian, Malcolm, and Nolan had come together in Gillian's Mazda and she parked in a corner spot behind the law offices. Most of the lawyers in the city had grouped together in this district near the courthouse. Heller & Associates was doing quite well apparently. They had their own building with customer parking. It was a 5 story brick establishment with a small lobby on the bottom floor. The secretary directed them to a coffee station and had them sit in large leather couches to wait.

Malcolm felt like the couch swallowed him and made him feel small, he noticed Nolan did not sit down and instead wandered the small lobby touching anything that was left out. He sighed as he watched his new sales VP pick up the lobby phone receiver and listen for a dial tone before hanging it back up. He began to worry that Nolan would page someone or begin punching in extensions but instead he had headed over to a fake tree and was stroking the leaf material as though judging the quality. Gillian was engrossed with her phone punching out a message with her thumbs so rapidly Malcolm was almost jealous of her slender appendages that could easily hit only one letter at a time.

The elevator binged and a woman in a black skirt and suit jacket stepped out, high heels clicking across the floor as she strolled over to them. She held a laptop under her left arm like a purse and reached her right hand out to Nolan to shake his hand.

"Nolan, good to see you again. How have you been?" she asked.

Nolan ignored the offered hand and went in for a full hug. "Beck, good to see you! I've been great." Nolan stood back and held her shoulders as though supporting her, "How have you been? How's business? You look great, whatever you are doing, you're doing it right." he didn't give any time for replies.

Malcolm noted Beck was smiling and assumed she had come to know Nolan's behaviours from previous meetings. Her hair was pulled back into a blond ponytail and he guessed she was in her early 30s. When she had come out of the elevator she looked perturbed and all business, but Nolan's greeting seemed to soften her mood. "You know the business, sue everyone you can, hire everyone you can't. We've been growing like crazy and just leased another building in Guelph. We're going to open a second office there."

"Nice!" said Nolan with enthusiasm. "I want you to meet my new team, Gillian Cliff and Malcolm Joffrey." he waved his outturned hand to each as he named them. "We've created something you are definitely going to be interested in. This is Rebecca Stratton, IT director here, she basically makes the whole place function." Gillian and Malcolm were standing now and after shaking hands and exchanging pleasantries handed Rebecca their business cards.

She led them through a door marked Boardroom 2 and they sat around a large oval wooden table. The room had huge picture glass windows out onto the parking lot with hedges just visible below the window ledge. A projector sat in the middle of the table and Gillian connected her laptop to the HDMI cable protruding from it.

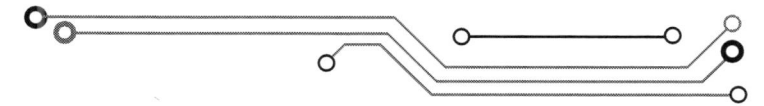

Malcolm thought the sales presentation went well. He went through the slides on the number of data breaches and ransomware attacks, and their effects on the businesses that were breached, then Gillian took over for the product side, really driving across the point that Log Driver had the best anomaly detection in cybersecurity at the moment. Nolan threw in colour commentary and a few comments directly about the legal business. Rebecca mostly paid attention, only distracted by vibrations from her phone a few times. At the end of the presentation she leaned back in her chair, her fingers steepled, staring at the large "Thank You" slide remaining on the screen.

"We can have a box installed for you by next week, Beck. Cybersecurity is critical right now, with new breaches hitting the media every day, you don't want to be the next article." Nolan was saying and Rebecca looked over at him. She leaned forward and put her elbows on the table.

"I'll be honest with you," she started and Malcolm took that as a bad sign, "I just got the budget for a full cybersecurity system and went with another vendor. They have a full suite of tools, from endpoint protection to vulnerability assessment. They have log anomaly detection, admittedly this looks better, but I can't see going back to the senior management to ask for more money for a single tool after what I spent on our new system. I'm just not seeing the value add here."

"I think your product is great for what it is, but I need a differentiator, something that would make the senior management team open the purse strings and this Log Driver just doesn't quite push the bar high enough."

Malcolm slumped back in his chair, but Nolan leaned forward. "That's great feedback. So you think if we had either a few more products or something no one else had, we could make them change their minds?" he said.

Rebecca sighed and flipped open her laptop, she plugged a USB dongle into the side of the machine and the screen lit up. "These are the dashboards we're getting from our current vendor." Her finger moved around the trackpad on the laptop and opened a web page. "You can see the amount of data we're already receiving. It's pretty spectacular. I'm not sure what you can add, but definitely if we were going to think of adding on to our current system, it would have to be pretty compelling. My team is already suffering from alert fatigue with the number of tickets this system is creating. We have paralegals that don't run their updates, lawyers that download too much porn and we have one legal secretary that doesn't just click on phishing emails, she keeps forwarding them to everyone in the office. We're swamped with what we have. I'd need to see something really innovative to think about adding another data point to the list."

Nolan was nodding as though he understood, his mind obviously spinning as he looked out the window at a blue BMW pulling into a spot just on the other side of the hedges. Gillian was typing away on the laptop, taking minutes for later review and nodding as well. Malcolm felt like he had to fill in the silence. "Thank you for your time Rebecca, we truly appreciate the feedback and insight."

"Oh, you're welcome." she said. "It seems like this Log Driver is a great product, but we just need a whole cybersecurity suite and dealing with individual vendors for each tool isn't the way we want to go about it. I really think you guys will do great once you have a few more products on the go. Maybe an antivirus and some vulnerability assessment tools would be the way to start."

"Well we won't take anymore of your time." said Nolan, standing and reaching out his hand. Gillian unplugged her laptop from the projector and closed it. "This has been a great meeting though, I'll stay in touch, Beck, and keep you posted on what we're up to."

"Sounds good Nolan. I have to run, apparently the lunchroom microwave causes the WiFi to drop in the 3rd floor men's bathroom and one of the partners 'works' from there." she sighed as she closed and picked up her own laptop, "I'll let you guys see yourselves out, Julie at the front desk can help you if you need anything." She walked quickly out the door, closing it behind her.

"Well that was a bit disappointing." said Macolm as soon as the door clicked.

"That's OK, it was insightful," said Nolan. "I knew they had just spent a wad on cybersecurity which is why I set this up. Find out what objections we're going to come up against with a friendly face. Beck has always been pretty blunt with me so I knew we'd hear exactly what the problem was. I have some ideas I'm going to work on for the flight back to California. I'll set up some meetings there as well, but I expect we'll be seeing some sales shortly. In the meantime you guys have your work cut out for you, which is why I wanted you here to get the info first hand. More products equals more business."

Malcolm struggled to maintain his composure. He felt every sales person wanted to sell things that didn't exist. Why not sell the product they already had, to people who needed it, instead of selling products that didn't exist to people who already had what they wanted. "First, you sell Log Driver to someone, and then we can talk about what comes next," he said.

"Deal!" Nolan exclaimed and had a huge grin on his face. Malcolm didn't like it.

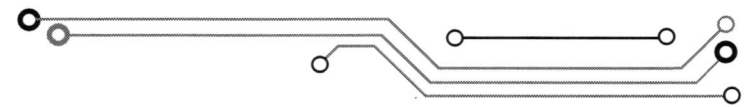

Nolan arrived at the San Francisco International Airport that night. As he drove south along Highway 101, he punched the voice button on his steering wheel "Send message to the family" he said aloud.

"What's the message?" the car replied in a pleasant woman's voice.

"Conference call tomorrow at 8 AM" he said loudly, over enunciating each syllable. The car had once sent a very private message to his dentist and he had got in the habit of being excruciatingly clear when speaking to it.

"Message sent." said the car.

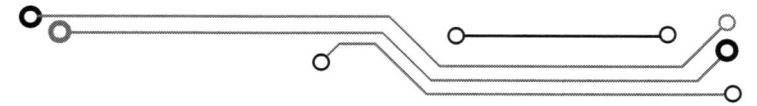

Malcolm was sitting alone in his condo the following Thursday. He had just got off a video call with his parents. His mom wanted to show him that Walter the pig dog could now sit on command. Well, as long as you had a treat in your hand he could sit on command. Malcolm thought he was gaining weight a little too quickly and wondered if the poor dog would make it through a year. He was sitting on the edge of the couch making a list of possible products they could use to enhance their portfolio when his phone rang.

"Nolan Walker" appeared in big white letters across the screen as it lit up. He sighed and picked up the device. It's clock showed 9:06 p.m. That would be 6:06 p.m. California time. He swiped his thumb across to answer. "Hey Nolan," he said.

"Good news buddy!" exclaimed Nolan's voice into his ear. "I've got a signed deal sitting on my passenger seat."

"What?" exclaimed Malcolm, "Seriously? That's amazing!" He stood up from the couch and began pacing back and forth in front of it. "Tell me everything!"

"Well once I got home, I called the Family." started Nolan. Malcolm was confused for a second then remembered the Sales Mafia thing, he was glad they weren't on video chat as his eyes rolled so hard he thought he could see the inside of his eyebrows. "And we were discussing this whole ... problem." continued Nolan, unaware. "Cybersecurity is huge right now. A ton of the gang is already selling different services and products in the field. 'Sandbag' Nick was saying he was the one who sold Heller & Associates. But this one chick had a great idea." Malcolm winced at the word 'chick' and began rubbing his forehead to ease the tension.

"Awesome." he remarked dryly, trying to get the story moving.

"So she came down to Sunnyvale and we went and did the sale together. It was brilliant."

"I don't know if we're financially ready to bring on another sales person right now." Malcolm said into the phone.

"Don't worry buddy, I'm taking care of this one through my commission."

"Did we have to cut our price for this? And you know you have a non-disclosure agreement, right?"

"Buddy!" shouted Nolan, "I'm a professional. You don't have to worry so much. It's not some kid out selling lawn services here. I had her sign an NDA before we went to the clients. And we didn't have to discount at all. Full monthly fee, paid up front for a year, I got a cheque right here made out to Dataffair."

"Well that's good news!" said Malcolm, feeling better. "Who's the client?"

"It's another law firm, out of San Fran. They do a lot of human rights stuff, but mostly criminal defence. You should've seen them. They were blown away by our presentation. I took all that feedback from Beck and totally leaped over any objections. And Summer Rainbow is a class act, she had them eating out of the palm of her hand."

"Summer Rainbow? What's that? Her mobster name?"

"What? Oh. I get it. No, no, she's just from California. She was awesome. Once Summer started talking, they were hooked, couldn't write the cheque fast enough."

"Wait? Go back a bit, Beck's feedback? I've been working on that. She said we didn't have enough products."

"Right! Or a way to differentiate ourselves from the competition. That's how I did it, I sold them Log Driver and our disruption product."

"What disruption product?" asked Malcolm, scared about the answer.

"Psychic Security Baby!"

Malcolm was worried he would pass out.

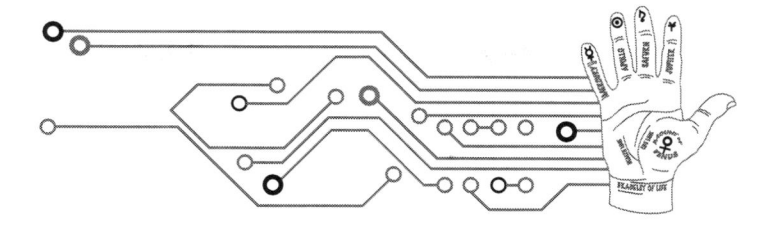

CHAPTER 0000 1010: LET THE GOOD TIMES ROLL

Malcolm hung up the phone and stormed out onto his balcony. The air was crisp and uptown Waterloo was beautiful with red and gold trees spread across the entire city. His balcony looked out at the new Google building. It was lit up brightly, it's coloured glass panels reflecting the street lights from below. At first he thought about flinging his phone into the city. Letting it smash somewhere down below. He wondered if he could hit the stupid Google building from here. He raised the phone clutched in his fist, would the shatter proof case he had spent so much on protect it? Then decided he should call Gillain first. She was probably sitting by a fire in Casa Vicky. She had named her old Victorian home downtown which was just another reason to be mad at her right now. He lowered his arm and spun around. Of course his condo was in the way, he couldn't see over to Victoria Park from here. He switched the phone to his other hand and jabbed her name with his finger.

"Hey Malcolm," came her voice before he even heard it ring.

"Wait 'til you hear what Nolan did!" he shouted.

"I heard some, he was just on the other line. He said you're mad."

For a moment, Malcolm's thoughts went to the fact that there is no "other line" on phones anymore, there isn't even a line. His focus quickly came back. "Damn right I'm mad! He sold a hockey helmet full of unicorn farts to some bleeding heart lawyers in California!"

"Yeah, that's what I heard." Gillian laughed, "Except I didn't hear about the gassy, one horned, horse. I thought you always wanted to be a disruptor?"

"I want to be a disruptor, sure, not be the one disrupted. He's going to make us the laughing stock of cybersecurity. You can kiss selling Dataffair goodbye, cause no one is going to be interested in us now, and I can't even imagine trying to go public if this hits the media. We need to do damage control here. We can fire Nolan and do a press release that he wasn't a good fit for the company and had taken his own direction." Malcolm wasn't breathing through the whole call and made a focused effort to inhale. Gillian took advantage of the break to jump in.

"Now wait a second. He did get full price for the sale and we do have ... something ... we can use for psychic security. Why not shore it up and make it into a product? Nobody's laughing at us yet. Risk and reward, remember?"

"But this is stupid. What industry exactly are we disrupting? 1-800 psychics and snake oils?" Malcolm could picture one of Nolan's ancestors riding around on a giant wagon with "Doc Walker's Miracle Remedy" painted on the side.

"It's not stupid." came Gillian's calm response over the phone. "People want to be happy and positive. We'll be making a difference in their daily lives if we can pull this off. People like being happy."

"People like ice cream, I don't see us pivoting into the Neapolitan market either. I explicitly told Nolan that he had to sell Log Driver first before we talked about other products."

"He did! Did you even hear the end of the story or did you get all worked up and block it out?"

Malcolm was ready to lash out, then remembered he wasn't mad at Gillian. All his work managing people and controlling his emotions came back to him. He inhaled through his nose, held it for four seconds, then slowly exhaled through his mouth. "I blocked it out." he sighed. "I was just so frustrated that he would sell something that wasn't even in our wheelhouse, let alone on our roadmap."

"We really mix metaphors, eh?" Gillian suddenly changed the topic. "Shouldn't it be 'Not in our drivers seat' if we are using roadmaps? Or we could switch 'roadmap' to 'navigation chart'. I mean in one we're on a boat and the other it's a car or bus or something."

"There are a lot of bus metaphors in tech." Malcolm said. "Get on the bus ... throw Nolan under the bus. I really think we need to look for someone more appropriate."

"Ok, hear the end of the story first. Yes, Nolan and Summer sold them the Psychic Security contract, but they also have a contract for Log Driver and BOTH at full price. It's not a huge law firm, but they have 200 people. He got $8,000 a month, paid up front for a year."

"Eight thousand?" questioned Malcolm, he wasn't sure he was hearing that right. "American?"

"Yup."

That was $96,000 of annual recurring revenue. If Nolan could start selling at that rate they'd hit the first million quick. Then it was all up and to the right, like a hockey stick.

"Wait. Why would they pay $4,000 a month for 'positive energy'? Who would do that?"

"You keep forgetting, most people, present company excluded, want to be happy more than they want money. This firm obviously puts a priority on their employees happiness and are willing to risk $4,000 a month to see if it helps. It's less than $20 per person per month."

"Wow." Malcolm was trying to picture spending $4,000 a month on something like an air purifier for the office or a healthy eating program. "You think this is a mental health thing?"

"I absolutely think this is a mental health thing," said Gillian calmly.

"Mental health is huge right now." Malcolm was staring at the Google building. He ran his hand through his hair, pushing it back, then adjusted his glasses. "Maybe this could be a thing."

"Yeah, maybe." said Gillian.

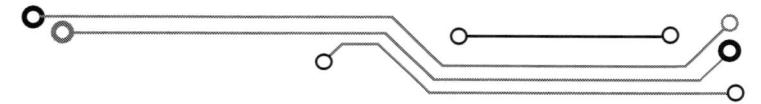

Jimmy was half sitting on Mike's desk Friday morning at 10:00. Neither Malcolm or Gillian had come in yet and he had pretty much just chatted with everyone in the office since he arrived.

"All I'm saying is that video games back then were more technology driven. First they made something, then they came up with a story to explain why you were doing it. Nowadays video games are art, they are story driven, you can reuse the same tech, heck even the same code and only change the story. The independents are the only ones still relying on tech demos as game play. I mean what the hell was Pac-man even doing in that maze? And ghosts? C'mon, they were just easy to draw."

"Frogger had to get across the road to mate. That's a story. He has motivation." said Mike. He was leaning back in his chair, his hands folded over his stomach. These were conversations he enjoyed.

"Frogger! Pssh." he turned his head so as not to spit on Mike. "Why was he even on the wrong side of the road? What's his story? He had to get there somehow, it's not like he grew up on the sidewalk all alone."

Malcolm appeared at the door. "Jimmy, I have to talk to you, grab your coat, we can go for a walk."

Mike and Jimmy exchanged looks of concern. Malcolm's tone hadn't left any room for imagination. This was obviously a serious talk.

"See ya Mike." he said and pushed himself up to standing. "I hope." he added as he left.

He grabbed his coat, which was actually just a zippered hoodie that was big enough to fit over his other hoodie, from the back of his chair and headed through the kitchen. He saw Matt and Raj already in their own fall jackets standing around the doors with Malcolm. So it wasn't just him. Matt's jacket was unzipped and Jimmy read his shirt. "This is only a drill." it said with a drawing of a hand drill below it. He hoped that was true. Had their hackathon project been that bad he wondered as they headed out into the parking lot.

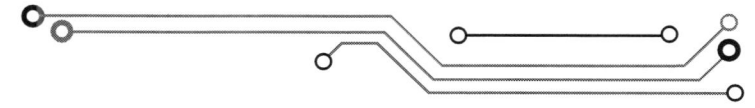

With no private offices, walks were how a lot of private conversations got done. Malcolm waited until they were at the far edge of the parking lot and on the sidewalk to begin. Everyone else was staying quiet, Jimmy looking at the ground as he walked, Raj staring off into space and Matt staring right at him.

"So here's the word guys," he started, "Nolan has gone and sold your psychic security project."

"What?!" they all seemed to exclaim together.

Jimmy was first to get something else out. "It's not production ready yet." They had all stopped walking and were just standing in a circle now.

"That was going to be my first question, what are the roadblocks to get this thing as a production unit? Can we mass produce that circuit board? And what does the code look like?" Malcolm was getting excited. He loved talking business.

"Wait!" said Matt waving his hands like he was a hockey ref and recalling the goal. "Why are we selling this? I thought you didn't really believe in the project, now you want to productize it?"

Malcolm brought up his hands and Jimmy thought he looked like a ref signaling 'checking from behind'. "I had a good talk with Gillian and she brought up the mental health benefits of the project and then I ... we decided that it was a direction that we wanted to go."

Jimmy grabbed his wrist with his other hand in front of his chest, making the refs 'holding' gesture. The other three turned to look at him. "I thought we were doing a hockey thing?" he explained, dropping his arms. "I have to say, I've seen Raj's code and it's ready to go. I have a contact in Guadalajara, Mexico that can do a short run of boards for us. We could easily build 10 of the psiPhones, and hundreds, even thousands of the emitter-sensors."

"True, remember each client needs lots of sensors but we probably only need one psiPhone for hundreds of clients." Raj jumped in. "The problem comes from routing the signals. Remember when we tried to push it through a network switch? It got dropped. So we can't route positive energy through the existing Internet infrastructure."

"Oh yeah, not a lot of positivity coming out of the Internet, that's for sure." said Jimmy.

"Crap." sighed Matt.

Malcolm pushed on his glasses. "So there's no way to run this to any office without putting in our own cabling? That would be crazy. I mean this first customer is in San Francisco, can we even do that one?"

"We could definitely do it locally. We'd have to put a Positech right in their office." replied Raj.

"We can't afford to pay a person to service one client," interjected Matt, "the margins on that would suck. I mean for the first customer it doesn't matter either way, but as we grow we'll need a single tech handling at least a hundred customers. Oh! If we did some timezone shifting, assuming they only monitor offices 9 to 5 local time we could potentially have a few hundred customers per tech. Unless they were really negative customers I guess ..."

"Whoa, whoa, whoa." said Malcolm. "Let's get this customer up, then we'll worry about the next hundred."

"And we're going to need a couple rolls of toonies." said Raj.

Malcolm just looked at him with his eyebrows raised.

"When we were testing we couldn't get any signal except through toonies." Raj shrugged. "And having custom toonies made would be more than $2 ..."

"Really?" commented Malcolm. "Our proprietary secret ... our intellectual property ... is that we're the only ones that know you can't transfer the energy through anything except Canadian two dollar coins ..."

"Yuup." said Jimmy. "At least it wasn't silver dollars."

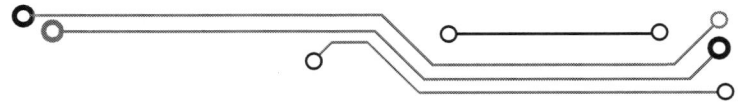

November was coming to Waterloo like a cautious swimmer. Dipping its toe into some snow once in a while before diving right into full winter. The air was cool, but the wind was light and a fall jacket was all you needed. It was cold, but it was a dry cold. The Dataffair office had been busy over the last few weeks. Sachet had managed to rig up a test centre for the new helmets and emitters. He switched the small check mark icon that usually appeared during a passed test to a happy face emoji and the failures showed an icon of Malcolm's face grimacing.

Mike had managed to create a device that could store the positive energy and emit it when needed. He called it Anode after the positive end of a battery. The software ran the energy through an analog compressor device and then cycled it live in a loop. Then it would switch the loop back to the output and emit it on demand. They had tried just storing the bits that made up the positive energy, but that didn't work. It was easy enough to convert the analog energy into bits and bytes, but when they converted them back to a signal it didn't create positive energy. It appeared it needed a higher fidelity of conversion. It was like converting a vinyl record to a digital file. The more bits you used the more details of the recording you would pick up. A CD only used 16 bits to sound exactly like the record for most people, but Mike had gone all the way up to 1024 bits with his conversion and still didn't get any positivity when he emitted it again from the anode.

It was Nasser that had come up with the analog solution of creating a long cable in a box and cycling the signal through it over and over again. They didn't notice any degradation of the signal as it looped around. Nasser presumed it created some kind of 'positivity field' that kept the signal at full strength. The switch would then route the signal back out of the Anode at any time, much like how a train switches tracks. Nasser had looped longer and longer cables until they found they could store 8 hours worth of energy. This would allow the Positech to come in and fill up the Anode with energy and it would be able to run all day. They each tried putting on the psiPhone and filling the Anode to see how long they would need to have a Positech connected each day. Gillian wound up being the fastest, she wore the helmet for ten minutes before the Anode binged a bright tune alerting her that it was full.

Malcolm was crunching numbers. A single Positech could fill 6 Anodes every hour. He didn't think they would be able to sustain positive thoughts for 8 hours, but he figured with breaks and down time, they should be able to do half of that. So a single Positech could handle 24 emitters each day. They had found that the emitters caused a Positivity Perimeter (Jimmy had coined that one) of about 1,000 sq. ft. The law office they had sold was about 5,000 sq. ft. So on a conservative side one Positech would do 4 law offices, or $16,000/month in revenue. He frowned. By the time he rented office space and paid them, the margins were much too slim. He really wished Mike had been able to convert whatever this positive energy was into a digital signal. If digital worked, it would mean they could figure out a way to copy it. They could just have computers create whatever bits were required and send them on. "Just eliminate the people," he thought as he closed the spreadsheet. He and Gillian were flying to San Francisco tonight to see some office space tomorrow. He wanted to talk to Mike and see if he could psych him up before he left. He was sure if anyone could digitize positivity, it was Mike.

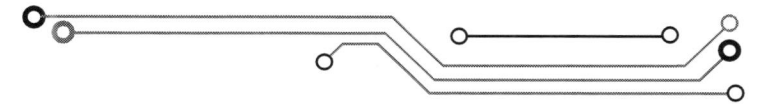

Gillian and Malcolm flew out of Pearson airport on an Air Canada flight at 5:45 p.m. Although it was a five and a half hour flight, they landed in San Francisco at 8:25 p.m. thanks to the time change. Nolan met them in the airport. They hadn't eaten before flying so Nolan led them to the Mission Bar & Grill, a restaurant right in the airport where they could talk and eat before he took them to their hotel. He chatted nonstop about his drive up from the valley until they got seated. They chose a place close to the window as Malcolm enjoyed watching the planes.

"Great news!" he exclaimed as he was pulling out Gillian's chair. Malcolm couldn't decide if he was being aggressive or chivalrous. "Summer has hooked us up with a guy she knows for the first Positivity Technician position. Hey, that rhymes!" he laughed.

"We're calling them PosiTechs, remember? Is his name Cloudy Day?" Malcolm snorted.

"Hey! You gotta get over that Malc. This is San Fran, and we're going to be doing a lot of business here. You need to open your mind to new ideas. The world is changing. Bob Dylan called it back in the 60's." Nolan took his own seat.

Malcolm didn't think Bob Dylan ever wrote a song about naming your kids after weather patterns. He felt Nolan was the one that had to realize that the times; they were a'changing. "Sorry." he said, "So tell us about this candidate."

"Well," said Nolan, rubbing his hands together over the table, "his name is Milo and he runs his own business currently, but he's willing to contract with us in the beginning and then see how it works out."

"Contract is good." nodded Gillian. "What's his business?"

"Oh, he's right into the gig economy, he does a lot of different things. Summer is actually a client of his." Nolan paused while the waitress collected their drink orders. Malcolm got a Perrier, Gillian ordered a pint of Blue Moon Belgian White and Nolan asked for the same.

"So what does he do for Summer?" asked Malcolm.

"She says he's the most positive guy she's ever met. Always wearing a big smile and great for bringing you up when you're down." Nolan looked out at the runways, "Great views here."

This time Gillian asked, "And what exactly does he do for her?"

"Oh you know, he does Yoga stuff I guess, or Zen ... I'm not up on all the new age stuff. He cleanses her aura for her and checks for ghosts and things like that."

Gillian laughed and Malcolm's eyebrows soared past the rims of his glasses. "Did you say checks for ghosts?" He managed to get out.

"Well he's one of these, paranormal investigators. You know, they go around and make sure your house or stuff isn't haunted. A lot of people are using them, you know. And it's not all he does, he's a life coach and a psychic and apparently is doing quite well in the triple P business."

"Oh gawd." said Malcolm.

"Well he does sound interesting." smiled Gillian, "But I have to ask, what's triple P?" she turned her head on an angle, trying to piece it together.

"Oh, yeah, it stands for Professional Plutonic Pal. It's becoming all the rage in the valley. You get all these computer geeks that can't make friends right?" Malcolm winced. "Or maybe they don't have time, so they hire a buddy. Someone they can text or play XBox with or whatever." Nolan shrugged. "You guys don't have that yet?"

"Not that I've heard of," said Gillian.

"Wow." said Malcolm, staring off in the general direction of the window. "I could actually see that. I wonder if anyone has organized that. Be like the Uber of friends."

"No idea." said Nolan, "but you have to figure, if he's making a living at this stuff he has to be positive. We don't want to let whatever he's doing now stop us from hiring him for this position."

"True," said Gillian smiling. "And for contract work, we can have him come in, fill the Anode quick and then clean out any evil spirits in the office."

"You mock," said Nolan. "But look at what we're selling!" He spread his hands.

"We're selling bullshit." said Malcolm.

"Bullshit as a service!" exclaimed Nolan and they all laughed.

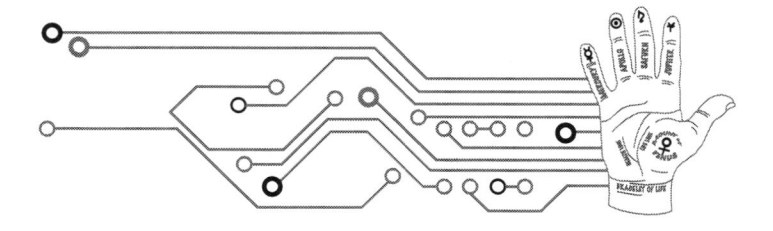

CHAPTER 0000 1011: ENTER MILO

Nolan arrived at the Marriott bright and early. Malcolm was glad to see him, since Nolan had promised to take them out for breakfast. The hotel was only a few blocks from the office space they were looking at so they had decided to walk. They were in the Financial District of San Francisco and the buildings were an eclectic mix of 1920s architecture with modern glass towers right beside them. The street car rolled down the centre of the street and eBikes were lined in bike stands that you could unlock with your phone. You were charged by the minute, but could leave them wherever you liked. Malcolm was wearing his usual khaki shorts and button up, Gillian had opted for a Xena T-shirt with an unbuttoned lumberjack shirt over top and black jeans. Both had deck shoes on, but Malcolm's were the standard denim blue with white sole and Gillian's were checkered DC skateboard shoes. They walked a few blocks and Nolan turned into a storefront of one of the older 1920s buildings. Malcolm sighed seeing it was a McDonald's. He thought dreamily of the rows of breakfast sausage he'd seen back at the hotel.

"Barton & Paget are in the building next door," said Nolan.

"There's actually space for lease in this building too and they're attached. But I don't know all the codes for running cables between them." He stepped up to the till and began his order.

Malcolm and Gillian both added their orders and they took a seat in the small dining area.

"Keeping it simple seems like the best plan," said Gillian. "Exactly!" exclaimed Nolan, "We've got the space for an hour, so we can really check it out. Afterwards, I arranged to meet Milo at Yerba Buena Gardens, I think you'll like it there."

"Who's Milo?" asked Malcolm.

"The guy I was talking about yesterday. You're going to love him. Even on the phone I could just feel the energy coming out of him." Nolan made a gesture like he was ripping his own intestines out and Malcolm wasn't sure he was portraying the image he was hoping for. Gillian looked at him and laughed in spite of herself. She shrugged and the look on her face calmly said "What are you going to do?" Malcolm couldn't understand how she was so laid back and grimaced a response. He felt like he was in the right place for Grimace.

Two trays were laid out for them and their food dropped on top. Malcolm carried one and Gillian the other, Nolan led the way to a table. They finished breakfast quickly, mostly talking about the neighbourhood. Malcolm felt it was declining, but Nolan assured him the Financial District was where they wanted to be. After cleaning up their garbage and dropping the trays on top of the bin, they headed next door to look at the office space.

The real estate agent let them in and said she'd be back to lock it up in an hour. They just had to close the door behind them. Malcolm looked at the size of the space and immediately wondered if they were wasting their time. If they took a three year lease on this place and this whole positive energy thing went nowhere they were left holding the bag. "What do you think?" he asked Gillian.

Gillian wandered across the worn Berber carpet, exploring the open space. There was a reception desk left behind by the previous tenants and you could see the lines in the carpet from cubicles. Wires hung from missing ceiling tiles and the windows were small, not the floor to ceiling style that became popular in the 80s, but there were lots of them. The building was old, but it certainly had character. You could see the original ceiling up through the missing tiles, although it was now covered in pipes and cabling. The window trim appeared to be original even if the windows weren't. Looking out, you could see a modern skyscraper across 2nd Street. Below the front windows was the bustle of Market St. "I like it!" she said. She was already picturing the style of the office. To keep positive energy flowing it would be totally unlike anything anyone had built before. You'd need artists more than contractors and interior designers more than office planners. She was excited. "How about you?"

Malcolm felt depressed. The drab colours on the walls, the dirty carpet, the derelict furniture, not even worth moving or selling. How could anyone be happy here? "What kind of access do we have to the Barton & Paget office?" he asked, turning to Nolan who was leaning at the window staring down at the street.

"Oh," he said turning around, "they are just one floor down, lots of access. I think we may even share the bathrooms with them."

"There's not a washroom on every floor?" asked Gillian.

"Oh there is," said Nolan, "but not two. So it's men's and women's every other floor." He made an imaginary stack of blocks with his hands. "Believe me, we're not going to find anything else for this price in this area. I think it's brilliant. We can put a little sales office in here too. Some hotel desks for the family."

"How many offices are in this building?" asked Malcolm.

"Um," Nolan began to tick off his fingers one by one, "16 I believe, and we'd make 17. Some take the whole floor but a lot just have half a floor like this. Mostly accountants, lawyers and investors."

"Alright, you make those sales and we'll build you a dream office here." Malcolm smiled.

"Oh, I can do that." Nolan smiled back with a hint of drama, "I already sold another one."

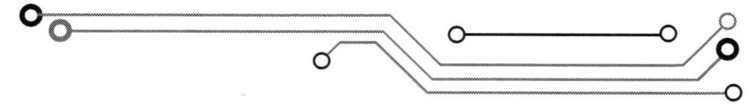

With almost $100k in annual revenue on the line, Malcolm and Gillian decided getting the office was the right thing to do, they discussed the terms as they walked over to Yerba Buena Gardens. They were to meet Milo at the Martin Luther King, Jr. Memorial. It was a broad, concrete waterfall on the southeast side of the park. This meant they had to walk across the entire 5 acre park to meet him. Gillian brought up a picture of Milo from LinkedIn on her phone and shared it with Malcolm. He had a mass of curly hair that was loosely pulled back into a ponytail that hung down past his shoulders. He had glasses with steel octagon frames on in the photo and a huge smile that took up almost half his face. Surrounding the smile was a short beard that looked like it could use a trim, some hairs obviously outpacing their associates. His nose looked like it had been broken at least once with a hard turn in it just below his eyes and a bottom that spread wider than might be expected.

Gillian scrolled through his massive list of experiences. Almost every position had an impressive title; President, CEO, Guru, Ninja, Rockstar. All the tropes were there. Malcolm pointed out that there was no last name on the profile which Nolan confirmed. Milo was just Milo.

And then they saw the live version. He was sitting on the concrete edge of the waterfall, cross legged with his hands upturned on his knees. His eyes were closed behind the glasses and they hesitated a minute before Nolan touched his shoulder. "Milo?" he asked.

Milo's eyes popped open and he went from on the ledge to hugging Nolan so fast Gillian didn't see the transition. "Nolan!" he shrieked, "It's so good to meet you in person." It quickly became the Milo show as he didn't wait for responses to any questions. "You must be Gillian and you're Malcolm! Nolan told me all about you." he said, hugging them in turn. They both noticed what they would call a body smell. It wasn't full out body odor, but more like a generic human smell. "Did you guys look at that office this morning? Nolan was telling me about that. Was it awesome? On Market St., downtown San Francisco!" he exclaimed, throwing his hands out, "How could it not be great!? That's so good. That's totally awesome. You guys are awesome." He stepped back to view them from a distance Malcolm appreciated. "I love this look, total odd couple for the founders, am I right? Casual geek chique for him and hardcore nerd for her. I love it. I'm totally going to call you Gap and Spencer's behind your back." He laughed with his whole body and cupped his hand on Malcolm's shoulder. Malcolm shuddered involuntarily, but Gillian laughed, she had actually bought the Xena T-shirt at Spencer's and was pretty sure everything Malcolm owned was from The Gap.

"So you're ready to give us your positive energy to spread joy throughout our clients?" she asked.

"Ready? I was born to do this job. I mean here I am juicing up everyone in this park for free and I could get paid for it?" he laughed again. "Just kidding, I'm still going to spread joy for free everywhere I go, it's my nature, man." His face got serious and he pointed from Gillian to Malcolm, "You gotta follow your nature. It's not natural not to be natural if you know what I'm saying."

Malcolm was a bit overwhelmed by Milo's nature. He felt like it wasn't natural. "What if it's in your nature to be an asshole?" he quipped.

"No man, that's not your nature, that's the effect of outside influences. People like to claim they are nasty by nature, but it's not true. I feel for them, man. But you're not like that! Look at you, I can see some total blue's in here." Milo began picking the air around Malcolm, like an ape pulling bugs off it's brethren. "And you have some green's, I mean, I can totally see you're shielding your aura, but man, there are no bad colours for aura. Like, there is no evil colour, that's how I know that everyone's nature is to be good, maybe in different ways, some artistic, some wise, some loving, but there isn't a negative aura, that's not even a thing, man." "Interesting." said Malcolm, stepping a little back, even though he wanted to say, "Well, you're crazy." and walk away. Instead he said "If Nolan explained to you what we are looking for, can you come up to Waterloo and try charging our positivity battery, we call it the Anode. We'd love to see how you do. If you can fill it at least as fast as Gillian here, then you're hired. We wouldn't need you for very long each day in the beginning, but hopefully it will grow."

"For sure, man. Gillian here is all reds and oranges. I'm less red and more pushing into the yellows, so I'm sure I got this. She's got the passion and I got the joy, it's going to be brilliant."

"Thanks!" said Gillian, quite happy with her red assessment, whatever that meant. "We'll hire a contractor to get the office ready while you learn the ropes. I'm sure the team's going to want to show you how to set everything up for when you are on your own. I have a very positive feeling about this." She leaned on the word positive, but no one seemed to get it, even Milo just smiled politely.

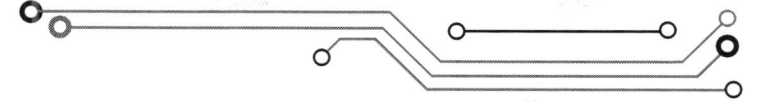

Milo arrived in the Waterloo office like a tornado. No one was left untouched as he spun from desk to desk, reading auras, patting backs, and hugging. Malcolm remembered Nolan's first day, it seemed so tame now. Everyone seemed to like Milo though. He saw him talking to Cheryl at her desk, he even saw him doing something that looked like a chiropractic move on Mike. No one touched Mike. Sachet and Nasser were setting up the Anode for the test. Since his trip, Malcolm had been thinking about patents. Could you patent positive energy? He didn't think so. Probably just their extraction and transfer methods. Surely, you can't patent a Toonie? If it was going to sell as well as Nolan believed he wanted something in place that stopped everyone from doing it. He thought maybe they could license Positivity Storage Brokers across the country. That wouldn't reveal how they got the positivity in the first place. That might be an idea ...

"You can't buy happiness", his mom had been telling him at Thanksgiving. Now you could lease it for $4,000 a month.

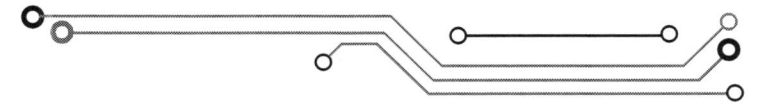

Sachet was placing the psiPhone on Milo's head. They were having an issue getting it over his big hair. "What if you don't like who you are?" Sachet was asking. They had been talking about Milo's "be yourself" philosophy.

"Dude, chances are, if you don't like who you are it's because you're not being you." He drew an imaginary line in front of him with a finger as Sachet wrestled with the helmet. "This is your life right, born at the beginning, go meet Santa Claus at the end, right? If you start trying to be someone you're not, or you go making decisions that don't follow your beliefs, you are straying from that line. Then what are you? You're just a one sided triangle, you know? That doesn't make any sense. You are a line, man! Live that line! Be ... that line."

Sachet was pushing curls through the vents in the helmet to try and get it to sit right. He was understanding hockey hair now. "So it's like destiny or fate you are saying."

"No, no man. If you are true to yourself, then you'll follow the line. It's not destiny, you can make a bad decision, you can stray from the line, but then you aren't being yourself. But you can always go back to your line, you just gotta be honest with yourself. Get it?"

"Interesting. In software testing we have what's called the 'happy path'. It's where you write tests that only validate the code that's expected to run and where it's expected to lead. Now in testing, we have to check every path so that we know what happens when things go wrong. But basically you are saying, stay on the happy path."

"Brilliant buddy! Exactly. And not everybody's happy path is the same. You don't want to be out in the weeds of life. Stay on the happy path. I like that, can I use it?"

"For sure!" said Sachet, grinning widely. He felt like he had helped and maybe made a friend.

Nasser came over with the cables to connect the psiPhone to the Anode. He stared at the flocks of hair standing straight out of the helmet vents and raised one eyebrow. "That looks totally ridiculous," he said quietly.

"Dude, don't judge." Milo laughed, "I'm going to ask Jimmy if we can come up with a new design, man. Maybe a headband or something."

"Ok, I'm going to have to push some of this out of the way to get access to the ports, don't mind my hands."

"You can stroke my hair all you want. I don't mind."

Sachet smelled his own hands behind Milo's head and winced. He headed to the washroom, "I'll get everyone and tell them we're ready."

After Sachet had done his 20 seconds of hand washing he gathered the team around Milo. Everyone wanted to see if he could beat Gillian's time, including Gillian. Matt was in a shirt that said 'man which' in computer lettering with a picture of a Sloppy Joe sandwich below it. "I'm putting $20 on Milo crushing it." he said.

"$20 Canadian?" replied Milo, keeping his head still and just moving his eyes towards Matt. "Is that even worth turning the machine on?" He laughed.

"OK, here we go!" said Sachet. He typed a short series of commands and the psiPhone lit up and began filling the Anode. Everyone watched the progress bar display on Nasser's laptop until at 3 minutes the Anode beeped, signalling it was full.

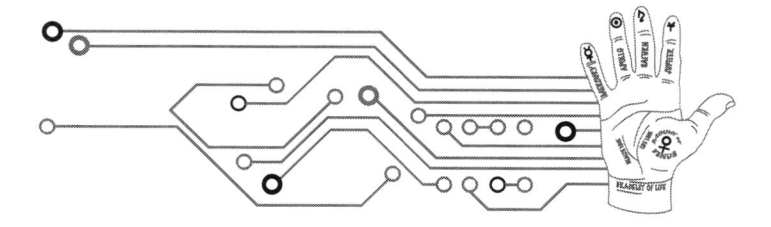

CHAPTER 0000 1100: PUSH THE TURBO BUTTON

Christmas came to Waterloo like a blizzard, literally. Dataffair had shut down their offices since their clients were closed anyway. Snow had come in on Sunday and there was no way people would have got to work even if they had been open. Gillian had driven back to Niagara on Friday night, fighting the University holiday traffic to get to family. Niagara had less snow due to its proximity to Lake Ontario, but the ground was covered in gorgeous packing snow, perfect for tobogganing and snowmen. Her dad had used one of the tractors to clear the laneway and piled the snow high all in one place. Her older brother and his wife had come in from Toronto with their kids. Her younger brother, his wife and their kids lived in the hired man's house just next door.

Gillian was in her prime. Out building a giant snow fort with her nieces and nephews in the snow pile. They had created sled runs around the outside and secret passages through the snow block walls. The kids were joyous, bits of snow clinging to their scarves and toques as they threw snowballs at invisible attackers, then diving for cover inside their secure fortress.

It was while huddling on a bench of snow with the kids shouting and flinging snowballs at imaginary monsters that Gillian realized she was going to leave Dataffair. Nolan was starting to bring in enough sales they should be able to attract a venture capitalist. Malcolm would be happy taking over as sole owner. She would see them through the winter, but she might start looking for property while she was here.

She belonged here, in Niagara. She could get some property, with an old barn, maybe 10 acres in Pelham, heck, maybe even Dunville (but probably not). She would join the church there and meet the people and just live the simple life. Maybe help her brother and dad with the farm when she wanted, open that flea market stall and just relax. She had really enjoyed setting up the office in San Francisco. Maybe she'd start an interior decorating business. She'd had enough of tech companies, exponential growth, and spreadsheets. She didn't regret having done it, she had needed to. But it was time to come home.

She smiled to herself when suddenly her face was washed with snow from a mitten that came out of nowhere. She stood up and giggles erupted everywhere. She roared and began a Godzilla style walk towards the scrambling children.

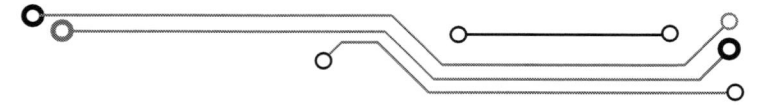

"What about Gillian?" Malcolm's mom was saying through their video chat. Malcolm had a spreadsheet open showing the cost of an Anode and its drain rate. They were about to hire another PosiTech and he was doing an analysis if they should have them and Milo in at the same time or worked them in shifts.

"Mom. Stop." he muttered, being careful to keep his face straight since she could see him even if he couldn't see her.

"She's your partner right? And she seems so nice. Did you know she sent us a Christmas card, look at it." She held up a paper card that was intricately cut into a Christmas village scene. "I think it's hand made, that's a lot of work.

Malcolm flipped back to the video chat to look at the card. "Mom, they have a machine that does that now. It's called a Cricut." His mom appeared to be sitting at their round kitchen table. He could see a 1950's beach poster hung on the wall behind her.

"Well I still think it's sweet." she bemoaned. "Oh, wait until you see Mr. Trotsky" her body disappearing below the table and camera. She was soon upright again hefting a very overweight bag of wrinkles.

Malcolm shook his head and his eyes went wide. "What have you done to that poor animal?!" he said. "And I thought his name was Walter."

"Oh it is. Walter Trotsky. He trots all the time on his walks."

"Are you sure he can walk?"

"He's not that big."

"Well he'll certainly make a good meal for one of your alligators."

"That's not nice Malcolm James. And there aren't any alligators around us."

Malcolm decided it was time to change the subject now that his middle name had been hauled out.

"The good news is mom, the company is doing really well. We're bringing on more staff and our office in California is up and running."

"But you still can't come here for Christmas?"

"That's exactly why I can't come down mom. We're ramping up. This is the crazy growth period. If things keep going like this, I could see us going public in less than 5 years."

His mom allowed the dog to slide back onto the floor with a

thud. "Well let's just hope we're all still alive by then." she said, staring directly into the camera. "Your dad and I are going to fly back in May to see everyone. I'm assuming you'll be able to take a break from your very important business to take us to St. Jacob's and tour us around."

"Absolutely Mom. Looking forward to it. You don't need to worry, this is exactly where I'm supposed to be and I'm doing exactly what I've dreamed of."

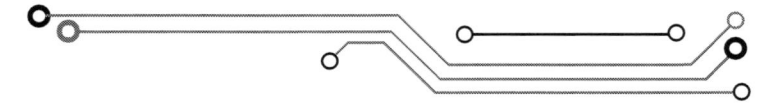

Boxing day was a Wednesday. Everyone in Canada had two choices of things to do, line up for sales first thing in the morning, or what Malcolm was doing and enjoying a quiet day. He thought he would watch a movie. He didn't watch a lot of movies, but wanted to catch up on the Marvel Universe. Apparently since X-Men they had made a bunch of really good ones. With the office shut down and only retail stores open, he figured it would be a quiet day. He had actually closed his laptop. He thought about moving it out of the living room, but then got worried he'd just have to go get it if the movie was boring. He was surprised when he got a video call on his phone. "Nolan Walker" appeared in big letters across the screen. Malcolm considered ignoring it, but then figured it would be nice to talk to someone today.

He swiped the answer button and was shocked to find Nolan shirtless brushing his hair. It appeared the phone was sitting on the bathroom vanity. "Um, hey Nolan," he said.

"Malcolm!" Nolan made a Fonzie-like move with his comb as he admired his hair. "Buddy, you NEED to get to Sunnyvale. We're about to rocket."

"You know this is a video call right?"

"What? Fucking voice assistants!" Nolan cried and his hands lunged to the camera. Malcolm saw nothing but black now so he switched off his own camera as well, rolling his eyes as soon as it was off. He placed the phone on the couch next to him since it was on speaker.

"Sorry about that," said Nolan. "When can you be on a plane?"

"Why do I want to fly down to Silicon Valley? You know it's Christmas right?"

"This is bigger than Christmas buddy! You know that guy that's suing the tree over in Georgia?"

"What? No."

"Oh man, it's big news. Apparently this tree owns itself, I don't know, I just saw the story. Anyway this guy slipped on one of it's acorns while he was taking pictures of it and is suing the tree. No lie. It's all over the breakfast shows down here. Don't you guys get American television?"

"Yeah, we get it. I must not be watching the right channel. But so what? What do I care if a guy is suing a tree?"

"Well, it's all over the news right? Human interest story. Guess who's got the case for the tree?"

"Barack Obama?"

"What? Barack Obama! The old president?"

"He is a lawyer you know."

"I didn't know that. But no. Not Barack Obama. It's Barton & Paget!" Nolan was obviously excited about this. Malcolm was beginning to wonder if he was on something.

"So?" he said and picked up his remote again and began scrolling through the movie covers on NetFlix. His phone sighed beside him and he looked at it.

"Malcolm. Buddy. I got a call from the IT director over at Barton

& Paget. They are going to be interviewed by Good Morning America tomorrow about how they are going to defend this oak tree. He told me that Vance Barton, one of the partners, is going to say that they got the case due to their Psychic Security system!"

"What?!" Malcolm sat straight up and grabbed the phone. He switched back on the camera. "Nolan, go back on camera. Are you shitting me?"

Nolan's face appeared on Malcolm's screen. He had a Hawaiian shirt on now but his smile was louder. "Malc. It's happening. When can you be on a plane?"

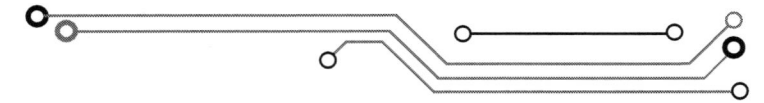

Gillian had met Malcolm at the carpool lot west of Burlington. They left her Mazda there and she rode in Malcolm's Tesla Model X. She ducked out of the way as the door swung open even though it wasn't necessary. She was looking at the large display showing traffic on the way to the airport. Looked like it would be an easy drive. She had her ski jacket and a colourful toque with a pom pom perched on the top. She pulled the toque off as she settled in and tossed it at her feet. Her hair was a mess of static. She looked at Malcolm's perfectly trimmed hair and realized what a benefit underground parking was. "So Nolan thinks we're going to be able to get some kind of TV coverage out of this?" she asked, even though she knew that was the case, she just wanted to hear Malcolm's thoughts.

"Yeah." The Tesla merged onto the 403 and came up to speed. "Apparently this guy suing the tree is becoming a huge human interest story down there. And something to do with our Psychic Security program is what made Athens-Clarke County decide to use Barton & Paget. I guess the County is the legal guardian of the tree or something …"

"Why are they even taking this seriously? Won't it be dismissed as a frivolous lawsuit or something like that?"

"Apparently all this press is bringing huge attention and tourism dollars, so they are rolling with it."

"Bizarre. But I could see Nolan getting us some press out of this. It'll be interesting to actually talk to a customer as well."

"True. I was looking at trade shows coming up next year and trying to figure out where we fit in. Didn't know if we should be at Black Hat, CEDIA, or the Psychic Expo." he laughed.

"Well, I'm glad we had a chance to talk alone anyway. I've decided that by the end of spring I'd like to step back. I'm not going to put pressure on you to buy me out. I just want to step away from daily operations."

"What?" Malcolm was shocked. He glanced over at Gillian and she was looking right at him. "Where did this come from?"

"Being back home." she said immediately. "I realized I want to move back. I'm done with tech for now. I'm going to sell Casa Vicky and buy a hobby farm."

"Wow!" exclaimed Malcolm. His head was whirling with what he would need to do to run everything by himself. They were in a growth stage and potentially this opportunity could lead to more growth. "It sounds like you have really made up your mind."

"Yup." she replied.

"Wow." he repeated. "Well can you stay on until I'm able to bring on some new VP's. I'm going to need someone to deal with Nolan for me!"

Gillian laughed. "For sure. No rush really, but I didn't want to suddenly hit you with it when I was leaving. We don't even need to tell the team yet. Just wanted to make sure you knew." She could see Malcolm was spinning. It was a good thing the car could drive itself if needed. Maybe she should've waited until they were on the plane, but she didn't like keeping things bottled up. Best to just spit it out.

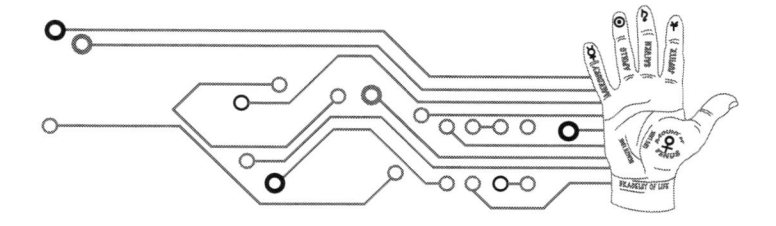

CHAPTER 0000 1101:
NO GOOD TREE GOES UNPUNISHED

Gillian and Malcolm walked into their office space in San Francisco. Malcolm hadn't been there since the updates were completed. He was stunned by the transformation. It was mostly open, with a few pillars that had been painted a soft blue. Along one wall were glass doors where he could see a series of Anode's spaced evenly in behind. They each had a tablet over them displaying details of their capacity and charge along with power usage, and other details. At the end of this glass closet was a server rack with a keyboard tray and monitor displaying various system details.

There were large, comfortable couches as well as floor pillows for sitting. The carpet was lush and Malcolm's first thought was static electricity. He noticed the pillars all had special outlets in them for fitting the connections of a psiPhone. Milo was sitting cross legged in the middle of the room on one of the cushions. The newly created psiPhone headband wrapped around his hair, cables tucked into his dashiki shirt to monitor his heart. His eyes were closed and his hands upturned on his knees. Malcolm was brought back to the day they had met just over a month ago. Light streamed through the windows and from Himalayan salt lamps placed on end tables throughout the room.

Soft music could be heard as well as what sounded like rain. Malcolm assumed it was some kind of white noise generator. A beaded curtain led to the sales offices at the front of the building.

"You did amazing on this!" he said to Gillian.

"Thanks!" Gillian had flown back in late November and managed the renovation as well as taken care of the decorating. Milo and her had spent quite a bit of time perfecting the Cosmic Positivity Center or CPC as Milo had called it. She wondered if Milo had influenced her decision to leave. He was so big on being true to yourself. She had really enjoyed decorating the office and shopping at the antique and sundry shops. She looked around the space with pride. "Nolan should be in his office. Let's see what he's got planned."

The bead curtain made rapid clacking noises as they passed through it. Nolan was seated at a desk facing them with the window behind him. "You know at first I thought that thing was stupid, but it really works well as an alert." he smiled. The sales side of the office completely contrasted the Cosmic Positivity Center. The walls were a light gray and motivational posters with golf courses on them hung everywhere. "We will either find a way or make one." was the first Malcolm noticed. Monitors hung on the wall showing sales projections, the marketing results and other statistics. The room had been divided with 6 foot tall walls breaking it into offices. Malcolm was reminded of a car dealership over an office building. There was a kitchenette along the back of the wall they had just passed through and a fresh pot of coffee was still filling. He noticed new sales reps in each of the semi-offices. Some even had two people squeezed in. Nolan got up from behind his desk and came out into the kitchenette area. "We're going to need more space soon!" He hugged Gillian and shook Malcolm's hand, "I really want you to meet Summer. She came on as Director of Sales, West Coast. Summer?" he spoke to a woman in the next cubicle. Malcolm wasn't sure what he pictured when he had heard of Summer Rainbow, but this wasn't it. She was wearing a beige power suit with black heels and belt. Her jacket shoulders were pointy enough to hurt someone. She wasn't tall and had the look of a powerlifter, not thin, but certainly not fat. She had thick rimmed, black glasses that reminded Gillian of Elvis Costello. Her hair was short and shaved completely on the sides. The top was held straight back with some sort of product where you could no longer see individual strands. Her eyebrows looked to be drawn on and impossibly long eyelashes shielded her brown eyes. She extended a hand to Gillian who was closest to her.

"Hi guys, I'm Summer, it's so good to meet you both." she smiled as she shook their hands.

"Summer's going to come next door with us. She knows the show runner and thinks she may be able to get us our own segment." said Nolan.

"Yes! You guys are hot right now and the world doesn't even know it." exclaimed Summer. "Psychic Security is the next big thing and we just got discovered. I'm sure once they hear about what we're doing, everyone in the country is going to be talking about it."

"Really?" said Gillian. "I mean we're just a start up, it's not like we've changed the world."

"Yet!" said Summer. "I wouldn't be here if I didn't believe you guys weren't going to change the world. I'm sure Nolan has talked to you about our elite group. The family is begging to get in on this. Trust me. This is going to blow shit up!" Gillian laughed, remembering she wanted that on their launch cake. She made the obligatory explosion noise and Summer joined in.

"This is going to be the biggest IPO ever." Summer shrieked.

"Don't you mean Psi.P.O.?!" Nolan made finger guns at Malcolm.

"Never say those words again." Malcolm grunted back at him.

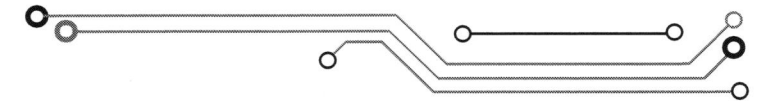

As they entered into the Barton & Paget office the first thing they all noticed was the plants. Malcolm didn't think he'd seen so many plants outside of a greenhouse. The lobby had wall to wall foliage. Extra tables and shelves had been set up to hold more plants. There were rubber trees, jade trees, bonsai, cacti, hoyas and palms. Most of the plants Malcolm couldn't recognize. Flowers of every shape and description were on display around the room. Leafy plants with yellow stripes down the center, tall palms taking up space beside doorways. A lemon tree that was pushing against the ceiling sat in one corner. The four of them marvelled at the amount of lush vegetation that was crammed into the room. Even herbs were growing in a planter box by the window. A large woman in a bright yellow dress was moving around the plants watering them and pulling off dead blooms. She turned as they entered, her watering can slightly splashing on the floor.

"Good morning!" she called out. She put the watering can on the floor and came over to hug each of them. "I'm so glad you could come. Nolan and Summer here, I know from the halls, so you must be Malcolm and Gillian, the savants that came up with this amazing product. I'm Tammy, office manager here at Barton & Paget. So good to meet you!"

Gillian rolled with it, giving Tammy a big hug in return. "It's great to meet you Tammy, we've been wanting to see a customer and get some feedback on how it's going."

"Oh my goodness, it's amazing. You must have noticed all the flowers."

"We did", said Malcolm looking around again, wondering how anyone could not notice the jungle they were standing in. If you wanted to hide an elephant in a room, this was the place.

"The plants just grow better here!" Tammy exclaimed. "It started with our office plants, but soon staff were bringing them in from home and the next thing you know ..." she passed her arm around the room. "We bring them in for a few weeks, then take them home. If they start to look stressed, we bring them back."

"Wow." said Gillian, her eyes wide, looking at all the flowers. "So you think they are growing better because of Dataffair?"

"Of course!" Tammy almost shouted. "The positive energy here is amazing. But I don't have to tell you that, your office must be incredible."

Gillian and Malcolm looked at each other. They hadn't actually thought of setting up a positivity center in their office. They had only been thinking of customers.

"Oh yeah." said Nolan, "It's what drives us to help others achieve the same results we're getting up in Canada."

"I've never actually met a Canadian before", giggled Tammy, "It's amazing how much you look like us."

"It is!" said Nolan, jumping on the comment before Malcolm could say something. "I can barely hear the accent anymore." He laughed and Tammy laughed, but Malcolm and Gillian just looked at each other, not sure what they were talking about.

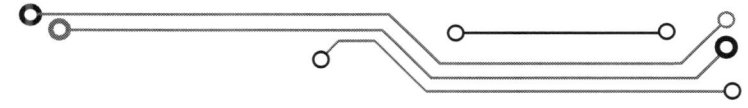

The camera crew had set up in a boardroom of the office. More plants were displayed around this room and the crew had placed a display of flowers and greenery behind a chair set out for the interview. They wanted to show the firm was all about the environment. A makeup artist was working on Vance Barton as he sat in the chair, adjusting details as the lighting was placed around him. The show runner immediately came over and hugged Summer, then Summer led her out into the hall. Gillian was impressed with all the gear just for a short segment, she wondered what Good Morning America cost per minute. She watched the crew for a bit before Summer returned and led them into a separate room with monitors all around. They could talk in this room without the sound being picked up by the microphone hanging over Vance's head but still see the action on the monitors.

"They are going to go live in a few minutes," Summer explained, her friend had stayed in the boardroom. "Susan is the show runner. She's going to talk to the producers after the interview to see if it makes sense to have you two on the show tomorrow morning. It really depends if he mentions you." Summer pointed at the monitor where Vance was mouthing "Red Leather, Yellow Leather" over and over. "Unfortunately, if that is the case, it means you may have to fly to New York tonight."

Malcolm sighed and Gillian put her hand on her hip. "Why did we fly all the way here then?" she said.

"I know, I know. Show business, right? They just prefer in-studio interviews, apparently this one is remote because Vance refused to do it otherwise." Summer shrugged, as they heard the crew start to talk rapidly. Everyone looked at the monitors. They could see Michael Strahan looking out at them. Everyone was listening on headphones but someone slid a control up on the panel so everyone in the room could hear.

"Our next story spans the entire country. You've no doubt heard of James Douglas, the man from North Carolina who is suing the Jackson Oak or Son of the Tree That Owns Itself, a famous oak in Athens, Georgia. He claims that he was tripped up by one of the tree's many acorns and that the tree is not maintaining a reasonable maintenance level of its property. We have with us the defence lawyer the county has hired to defend the tree, Vance Barton. Good morning, Vance." The main monitor switched to a side-by-side view of Vance and Michael. Malcolm noticed they always put the host on the right when they did that, he wondered why.

"Good morning Michael, it's a pleasure to be here," said Vance.

"This story has the country buzzing, we've heard of neighbors suing each other over trees, but never suing the tree itself."

"It is amazing," said Vance looking directly into the camera. "This tree has done nothing wrong. It certainly did nothing except what was natural for it, sowing it's seeds so to speak."

"Now the tree is in Georgia, but you are in California, how did you hear about this case and get chosen for the defence?"

"Well, we're a very special firm Michael. We do defence and human rights cases and in recent months we've achieved a success rate second to none thanks to our psychic security program." Summer turned to high five Malcolm and Gillian who were stunned that their program was just mentioned in front of millions of viewers on national TV. Malcolm found he couldn't close his mouth. Had he really just heard the term 'psychic security' used as though it was an everyday thing. Gillian was doing a little shimmy and Summer was outright dancing like the club was getting freaky.

"Psychic security? I've never heard of that, what exactly does that mean?" Michael was asking from the screen, no hint of his surprise. That guy is a professional thought Malcolm.

"Barton & Paget are what you call early adopters. We like to be on the cutting edge of technology. We're not talking about yogic flyers encircling the building and warding off evil spirits. This is actually a scientific process where we have a vendor that directs positive energy into our office when they detect any negativity in the air. Since we've started our program we've seen absenteeism sink to almost zero, our benefits program is looking at giving us a rebate, and we have had nothing but success." Malcolm's jaw closed. "Scientific" didn't seem like the right choice of words to him. This whole thing seemed crazy, he was suddenly hoping that Michael wouldn't ask the next question, but there was nothing he could do to stop it.

"Fascinating. Can we ask what vendor is providing this psychic security for you?"

"For sure Michael, it's a company called Dataffair and we were one of their first clients." Malcolm was already picturing the stories coming out, "Crazy company selling positivity" in all the papers, he was beginning to wish he had stopped Nolan from ever making this sale. Beside him Gillian and Summer were jumping up and down hugging, attempting to stay quiet for the people in the room, they were making whispered yells of joy. Nolan was pumping his fist, his eyes replaced by dollar signs. Malcolm was crossing his fingers that this story was about to be buried by some disaster, or a cat with a deformity that made it look like the reincarnated John Denver. Gillian was looking at him with joy in her eyes. He knew this was going to make them a lot of money, but he didn't want it this way. He wanted to be an Elon Musk, Steve Jobs or Jeff Bezos, instead he was going to be known as the next John McAfee.

His hopes for the story being dropped for the next big thing were dashed as he heard in the background, "… and I'd like to announce today, live, that we have just filed a countersuit on behalf of the tree against James Douglas for the harm he caused to the Jackson Oaks acorn on the tree's own property. We are suing for damages of ten million dollars, the acorn was cracked during the altercation and is considered unviable by our professional arborist. This poor acorn will never be the Son of the Son of the Tree that Owns Itself." Malcolm attempted to smile, but it just wouldn't come.

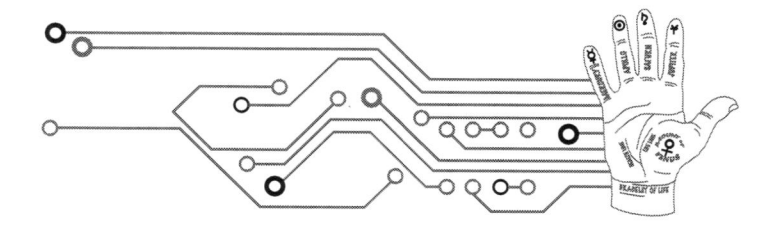

CHAPTER 0000 1110:
GO BIG, OR CAN WE GO HOME?

"Andrea is saying she had to bring up ten more web servers and a load balancer in our cloud." Gillian was saying. Her laptop was opened on the tray of her plane seat. Malcolm had his open as well. They were both connected to the plane's WiFi and messaging with the office. They were forced to call everyone back in from Christmas break. Most of the staff expected it after watching the show yesterday. Raj had been in the office when it aired and began emergency procedures to deal with the instant load on their systems. Messages were coming into their private chat system fast and furious. The co-founders had boarded the plane for New York shortly after the Vance Barton segment had ended. It was a flurry of activity as phones vibrated and binged to non-stop messages. By the time the two left, Nolan and Summer were organizing the 'family' to cover the major geographical areas of the states and began assigning leads to each. Malcolm and Gillian had heard from almost everyone they knew either by text or LinkedIn message but had time to respond to only a select few. They had promoted Milo to Cosmic Director of Transcendental Positivity Transference and Transformation (his choice) and told him to hire ten new PosiTechs.

"Cheryl is going crazy writing job descriptions. Mostly for jobs she's doing right now." Gillian laughed.

"We're going to need a finance team now." said Malcolm looking over at Gillian, he was stroking his chin, "and an HR team, and at least one trainer. I am impressed how fast Nolan had a team together."

"I told you he was good! He's doubling the price now, saying the old price was for beta customers only." said Gillian, she was getting the rush again. Thoughts of her move to the hobby farm pushed way back in her mind. "Oh, Cheryl is saying our phones are down, she's looking at an answering service to redirect all calls, we're being flooded." she said with excitement as her fingers flew across the keyboard responding to messages as fast as they could come in. "I'm going to tell her she owns it, whatever she does is right."

"Absolutely." said Malcolm. They had hired this team for a reason and he believed they were about to live up to the expectations he had. Mike was messaging that he was prepping the Anodes for different points of deployment so they would have redundant positivity across North America. His next message caused the chat stream to suddenly halt. It read "how r we networking these to distribute the nrg?" Malcolm leaned his elbow on the tray, his middle finger holding his glasses tight against his nose, staring at pocket in the seat in front of him.

"oh shit" appeared on the next line from Nasser.

They had no way to transfer the positive energy except in their own building in San Francisco. There was no way they could hire a PosiTech for every building across the globe. They didn't really have a product. Malcolm glanced over at Gillian as she switched over to the chat channel and read the messages and he could see the joy drain out of her face. Malcolm wondered if they could cancel the TV interview.

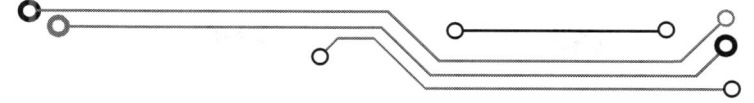

In Waterloo the office went from a zoo to a complete halt as everyone read the message from Mike. Only Cheryl in her reception area was still on the phone. One of the brainiacs in the back would figure it out, she thought. They had ABC on the large TV in the lunch room instead of the normal dashboards. They had replayed the Vance Barton segment 3 times throughout the day. In the back room Mike was standing at the door of his office looking over the desks, almost everyone was sitting in their spot staring at their screens deep in thought.

Finally Raj jumped up and went to a whiteboard. He wrote "WHAT WE KNOW" in block letters at the top. "Ok everyone, let's list what we know about the problem, then we can figure out how to fix it."

"It sucks!" yelled Jimmy from his desk.

"Something more constructive," suggested Raj.

"It's an analog signal," said Sachet.

"Right!" said Raj, writing "ANALOG" on the board. "What uses an analog signal and is distributed across the globe?"

"Power!" yelled out Matt, and Raj added that under analog.

"Phone?" asked Andrea.

"No, the phones have been digitally switched since the 80s" said Mike.

Matt looked at his one monitor as Vance Barton showed up again in a streaming video window. "Cable?" he said.

"No," said Jimmy, "TV went all digital in the 2000s"

"Wait!" said Mike, "They stopped transmitting analog signals, but they compressed the digital channels so that multiple channels could fit on the same analog frequency as one channel used to be. They would have freed up a ton of bandwidth, and who's to say they shut down all their switchers."

"Cable is run to almost every building …" said Matt.

Raj wrote "CABLE?" in big letters. "We need to make some calls." he said, "If you have anyone at a major cable company in your contacts now is the time to get a hold of them."

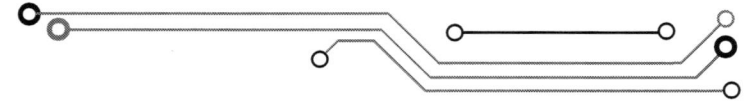

After they landed at JFK in New York, Gillian went shopping. She felt the clothes she had brought were too casual to appear on TV. Malcolm checked into the hotel and caught up with the team. He was overjoyed to hear about their cable plan, they just needed to pull it together. Nolan was manic with the rate he was booking sales calls. He wanted the service across the USA in 3 months. Word from Waterloo came that Cheryl was a wreck, Sachet was sleeping at the office apparently, and everyone else was just stressed. They all seemed excited for tomorrow morning though, which reminded Malcolm he had to be at the studio by six in the morning. He let his jet lag hit him, and flopped back on the bed. He was asleep before his brain could even register it.

Gillian was enjoying walking and remembering her first time in New York. She couldn't help but think this may be her last time. She turned off her phone while she shopped. The hustle of the city was doing nothing for her and the adrenaline was wearing off from the day. She went into a few shops and eventually pieced together a suit. It involved a long white shirt with cuffs that came down almost to her knuckles. A suit jacket she found at a vintage shop with tails that hung down to her knees. She wore the shirt untucked over her slax and it hung down to mid-thigh. With the heels she had on, it looked like it was bucking trends and stylish. She loved it and thought it was a fitting outfit to go out on a high note.

She checked her phone as she headed back to the hotel. There were texts and emails from almost everyone she knew. She wondered how many people actually watched Good Morning America and even knew her company name. There was an email from CityNews 570, the local talk radio station back in Waterloo. She'd definitely book them some time after the interview tomorrow. She had spent a lot of time in her car with talk radio back when she was commuting to Toronto. She thought about it and decided she wouldn't respond to any of them for now, her family had already heard what was going on and nobody else was a priority. What she needed now was sleep.

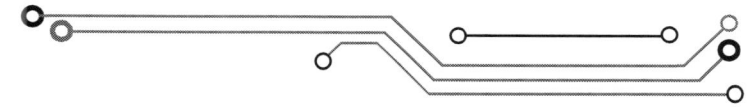

The co-founders were at the studio and in their makeup chairs bright and early. Malcolm had a Starbucks cup with his name on it and Gillian had picked up a coffee from the machine in the studio. Both had slept great thanks to the travel times, and would've slept more if they could. The energy was starting to ramp up now, it was a nervous, kinetic, energy. Sitting in the chair patiently while their hair and makeup were checked was just frustrating and both of them had their right knee bouncing up and down. It was the type of energy that made them want to run up and down the street, do jumping jacks or start a fight with someone. But instead, they had to sit still and wait until they were allowed back in the green room. They would wait there until their segment was lined up.

Summer's friend came in and gave them each a set of cue cards with a question printed on each. Gillian skimmed through them quickly, but Malcolm studied every question, pausing and thinking about each before flipping to the next card. He came to a card labelled "Ethical considerations?" and turned to Gillian.

"What do you think this question is about ethical considerations?" he asked.

"I don't know, maybe something about privacy." She was enjoying having her hair done up. So many days she just pulled it into a ponytail to keep it out of the way. Her mind was preoccupied by the image in the mirror. It felt like she was getting ready for graduation. Except instead of moving from scholastic studies to the work world, she was going to move from the work world to her own world, a moderate, relaxed life. She had put in the time and saved what she needed. She wouldn't be at the yacht club, but she could have everything she wanted. She was never one who wanted 'things', she was more of an 'experience' person. She created her companies because she enjoyed the work and adventure. Now that that was over, it was time to move one.

"I don't think we have any privacy concerns do we?" asked Malcolm, he went to push on his glasses and noticed they weren't there. The makeup artist was attempting to hide the crease between his eyes where they had sat. "I'm going to need my glasses," he stated.

"No worries, almost done here and you guys will be ready for show time. Break a leg." said the artist, sitting the glasses carefully back on his face. Malcolm's nerves were starting to twitch. He wanted to separate Dataffair from the tree lawsuit. If possible, he'd like to talk more about Log Driver and their cybersecurity business and avoid the whole positive energy thing, but he knew they were only here thanks to that. Perhaps he could talk about 'pivoting'. Lots of companies have done that. Amazon didn't just sell books anymore and Nintendo used to make playing cards, surely there was a way to lean on the 'security' side and remove the 'psychic' part. If Barton hadn't said it, it would be easier to spin. Malcolm knew the media loved to pick up on these things and he was pretty sure he was going to hear 'psychic security' a lot in the future if he didn't come up with a better description quickly. Something to do with mental health balance.

Just before 8:00 they were led to a set. Malcolm was glad to see a glass, bar height table with chairs. He didn't like the idea of nothing in front of him, he was pretty sure he'd spend the whole interview worried about if he looked fat or his fly was down. Now he was worried if the glass table would hide if his fly was down. Gillian grabbed the chair furthest from the camera before he had a chance. She hopped into the seat and seemed to be relishing all the attention. Malcolm climbed into his and smoothed his shirt. He had opted for a crew cut shirt with a gray sports jacket over it. His necklace was tucked in and he had his standard khaki pants. There was just enough of a black pattern threaded into the jacket that he felt it hid the microphone well. Gillian looked stunning, he thought. He felt they weren't too matched, but also didn't contrast too much. They looked like a team, maybe like a yuppie married couple that had lost the lust and romance of their relationship. He suddenly wondered if Gillian dated. Didn't she say something about hockey players? He had never thought about that before. He knew he didn't have time and just assumed she was the same.

Michael Strahan came over and shook their hands. "You guys ready?" he asked. Malcolm was stunned at how tall he was. Assuming everyone on TV was short, he expected Michael to be less than 6 foot, but he had to be 6 foot 4 at least. Michael took the seat opposite them after hearing their assurances. "This is easy, nothing to worry about. I'll ask some questions, you just look at me and answer like we're sitting at the coffee shop. The rest of the people here will be doing their jobs, so no need to worry about them."

Gillian turned and looked at the camera and declared loudly, "Fuck it! We'll do it live!" and Malcolm laughed. Michael just shook his head, apparently it wasn't the first time he'd heard that one. "Had to get that out of the way," said Gillian, blushing slightly.

"No worries, but let's have that be the end of the language." Michael winked.

Shortly Michael turned to the camera and began his introduction. Malcolm wasn't sure if he was on camera and did his best to cringe internally, when it started with "Yesterday, the world had never heard of psychic security ..."

Most of the interview went well. Gillian explained how the idea had come from a hackathon and what a hackathon was. Malcolm provided the numbers and information on how the positive energy worked, then a question came up that surprised both of them.

"Do you feel like it's ethical for these companies to force their employees to be happy?"

Gillian was the first to recover, "I don't think anyone is forcing them to be happy." Malcolm was concerned about the look on his face and trying to compose himself, they had never considered that they were forcing anything, they were just providing positive energy.

Michael continued, "I'm just wondering how this is different from pumping marijuana into the building or something like that."

"Well, this is a naturally occurring phenomenon. There are lots of people who emit positive energy all the time, that's who we hire as our Positivity Technicians. It's not unethical for companies to hire positive people and essentially that's what our service is. Positive employees, without the employee." Gillian was thinking on her feet, they had never considered anything like this.

"True, but you can also hire people with body odor, it's a whole different level to pump body odor into the building."

"True." said Malcolm, starting to get feeling in his face again. "But this isn't body odor, or anything untoward. This is more like pumping pure oxygen into the room, it has no ill-effects whatsoever. It's 100% positive, literally." He could feel sweat starting to build up in his armpits and back and was happy he'd chosen a jacket as well. The lights of the studio seemed to be brighter than they had been before. "If you are home watching TV and a stand-up comedian comes on and makes you laugh, is it unethical for that station to broadcast the comedian without your knowledge? As far as we know, this positive energy isn't even making you happy, it could just be triggering your own brain to make oxytocin, or serotonin. I don't think there's an ethical question here at all. We don't change people's personalities, the positive energy just makes them more sure of themselves and who they are." Malcolm didn't want to stop talking. He hoped if he talked long enough they'd have to cut to another segment before Michael could probe this any further. He was beginning to wonder to himself, what makes positive energy work? Does it affect the brain? Was it safe ... they hadn't had time to study any of this before Nolan had sold it. The time they could have invested in science was now gone, the cat was out of the bag so to speak, the company must go on.

"Well this is all very fascinating!" said Michael and Malcolm felt a shudder go through him, they were almost there. "I want to thank you both for your time, I'm sure we'll be hearing more about Dataffair in the new year, it sounds like an amazing service."

Gillian watched the tally light on the camera go off and smacked

Malcolm on the back. "We did it!" she said and gave him a hug. Malcolm dragged a hand down his face. All he could think was "What have we done?"

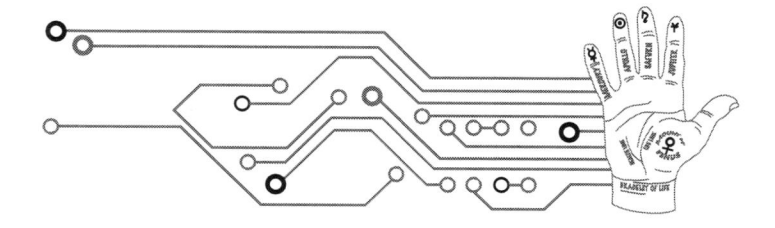

CHAPTER 0000 1111: MAKE HAY WHILE THE SUN SHINES

From January to June, Dataffair had grown at an immense rate. Malcolm only recognized about half of the over one hundred people in the Waterloo office. They had moved offices at the end of January, taking over an old Research In Motion building. Malcolm had an office on the second floor that overlooked the parking lot. He was amazed at the number of cars. Overwhelmed that they all belonged to someone that worked for him. Gillian had stuck with her plan and stepped back. She had been able to keep Casa Vicky and bought a hobby farm in Niagara. Malcolm hadn't gone to see it, but he'd heard from Cheryl that it had chickens, a few pigs and a single horse that had been named Step Lightly, a reference to the Log Drivers Waltz. Most of the others had stayed. Mike said he would have retired, but he just wanted to see what happened. Malcolm figured the stock options the rest had would keep them around until Dataffair had it's initial public offering. No one had time to vest very many options in the few years the company had been around and until IPO they weren't really worth anything anyway.

Malcolm was disappointed that Gillian had taken such an

inactive role and he didn't totally grasp her reasoning. This is what they had dreamed of, and just as it was coming true she had decided to remove herself. That didn't make sense to him. She could have been here with him getting all the attention and accolades. After their TV interview they had become celebrities in Waterloo and most of Ontario. Malcolm hadn't pushed her, as he didn't mind being the face of the company and was beginning to feel like he was a major player in the business industry.

The cable company had come through for them technically if not fiscally. They took $100 per month from every subscription, with a million dollar minimum, along with administration fees, hook up fees and anything else they could think of to pull money out of the venture. Still Dataffair had lit up all the major cities in the United States now and had Toronto, Montreal and Vancouver sales teams starting.

The new Chief Financial Officer, Julia Sykes, was looking into government grants from the States. The US was seeing a surge of innovation and jobs across all disciplines wherever Dattaffair had customers. It made sense that the government would support them in their endeavours considering the increased revenue it was seeing.

Offices that were using the Psychic Security product were seeing amazing growth and breaking new ground. Malcolm had done two tours across the States and was amazed at what some of their customers were achieving. He'd seen clothing that adapted to the weather by heating itself or opening air vents to allow a breeze to pass through and close them if rain started. Another customer had created a robot that replaced a seeing eye dog. An accounting firm had started over 50 training positions for people with no education, and provided them all of the schooling required to eventually take their CPA. It was truly unbelievable.

Milo now had 20 PosiTechs on his team and Dataffair had three more teams in Chicago, Seattle and Miami. They now had 7,500 customers set up and were signing new customers at almost 100 per day.

Malcolm had got used to the Psychic Security moniker and didn't even flinch when Time magazine ran a cover photo of him with "He knew this was going to happen!" in big letters. Most people were now calling the company Data Fair, and he was OK with that too. He had started wearing turtle necks, but not black, he wanted to separate himself from Steve Jobs, he wore coloured turtlenecks. All of them were solid and quite bright. Today he had a yellow one on with his blue jeans. He had noticed that since he had taken on this style, staff were able to pick him out better and he felt it was justified to continue. Every night they were at least mentioned on the Business News Network talking about where their IPO price might be, what their valuation was, and when it would happen. Malcolm found it a bit stressful, but considered it the "good" kind of stress. The money wasn't really important to him except for the legacy it created. Having the largest IPO in history would put his name up there with Jeff Bezos, Michael Dell and Bev Shepherd.

Once Nolan had found out they were broadcasting over cable he had come up with the idea of PostiviTV. He believed with all of the cable running to apartment buildings and houses everyone in America would want to sign up for a connection. Households would have their own positive energy device to keep everyone happy. The potential for that was huge and Malcolm had a team in research and development working exclusively on it. The issue was that the emitters didn't really have any proprietary technology in them. Anyone could reverse engineer it and figure out how it worked. It would be simple for someone to manufacture millions of them in China. The only thing they had right now was that no one had figured out the secret to collecting the positive energy and it needed to stay that way. Malcolm felt his team had lucked onto it. Hiring practices for the PosiTechs were extremely secure. They didn't want anyone to be able to duplicate what they were doing.

Malcolm's laptop started chiming and an Incoming Call window appeared over his audit report. It was his mother. Didn't she realize he had to work. He clicked the answer button and his mother's upper torso appeared in a new window. Walter was on her lap and he couldn't see her head as it was cut off by the camera. "Hey mom, tilt the screen back so I can see you."

"Hello Malcolm." she said and reached forward, the dog being squished as her camera moved first down, then up until he could see her.

"I was going to call you tonight mom, this can't wait?"

"Oh, I was supposed to know you were going to call tonight?" she scoffed, "I'm not the one with the psychic business."

"It's not a psychic business mom, we provide a positive atmosphere for our customers' staff to work in."

"Well that's not what the news says." she replied and gave him a look through the screen. "I don't know why you want to be a big wig if it just takes all your time. I mean how much money do you need?"

"It's not about the money mom. It's about putting my name in the history books. Creating a legacy."

"Oh, well let's hope the history books take care of you when you get old." she mocked.

"Was there a reason you called mom?" sighed Malcolm.

"Yes, as a matter of fact there was. It's Walter. He needs nasal surgery and I'd like you to take him into your care."

Malcolm tilted his head back to hold his eyes in. "Have you ever contemplated that animals such as Walter aren't meant to exist?"

"That's not nice." scolded his mother. "Lots of pugs need nasal surgery, it's not their fault."

"No," said Malcolm, "It's not their fault. Whatever it costs, I'll cover it. Get him fixed up well so he can breathe properly the poor critter." With that Walter blew chunks out his nose then licked his face to re-wet his nose. "Anything else I can do?"

"No, that's what I was calling about."

"Well since I have you, I wanted to let you know I'm heading to San Francisco to meet the team. We flew a bunch of the R&D team out there already to learn how the PosiTechs work and see if they can do anything to help them. I'm going to meet them there."

"I'd like to go to San Francisco," said his mother.

"Alright, I'll send tickets for you and dad."

"Thank you Malcolm." his mom said sarcastically.

"You're welcome mom. Talk to you later." He sent an instant message to his secretary to book his parents into San Francisco the week after he came back.

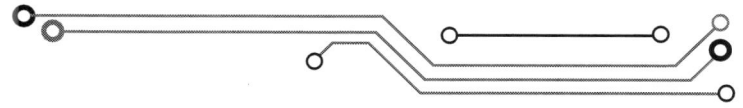

Mike owned a house in San Francisco and Jimmy, Nasser, Raj and Sachet were all staying there with him. Matt had been invited but wanted to stay in Waterloo with his family. The team had already been in San Francisco for a week and Malcolm was expected to join them for the following week. This was Saturday and the boys were kicking back.

Mike's basement had exposed beams painted white. A sitting area took up half the space and an arcade took the other half. The house was in the middle of the city and it took them 20 minutes to drive to the office. Everyone was overjoyed about not staying in a hotel for 2 weeks. Normally Mike rented the place when he wasn't here. He had originally bought it when he worked for a company in Silicon Valley, and had just kept it when he left.

The arcade was much smaller than his collection in Ontario but had all the favourites. Since it was the weekend they had decided to have a Golden Tee tournament. Anyone not currently playing either watched or played Ms. Pac-man or Tempest. They had stopped and bought beer and liquor on their way back to the house on Friday. The kitchen had been packed with snacks and a party sized pizza had just been delivered.

Nasser and Raj were deep in a discussion over the round coffee table. Nasser was explaining that the lack of a chicken pot cake was the irrefutable proof that pies were better than cakes.

"I don't understand why you work Mike." Jimmy was saying as he swiftly palmed the white spinning ball on the golf game. His shot on screen reflecting his movements sliced to the left around a bend in the course. "This place has to be worth what? Two and a half million?"

"Right around there," said Mike, stepping up to the machine and placing his beer on top of the cabinet.

Jimmy grabbed his own beer from one of the pub tables that Mike had placed between the machines. "Then you've got your farm." he emphasized the word farm. "That's gotta be worth two and a half. Why are you working? I'm telling you if I had one of these places and another two and a half million, I'd retire. Play video games all the time, do whatever you want. I'd be gone."

Mike spun the ball, his shot landed in the center of the fairway and rolled just up to the edge of the rough. Sachet, who was watching, whistled. "That was perfect."

"I've got two islands as well. It was a thing I was going through in the 90s." Mike shrugged. "One's up north off Manitoulin and the other is in BC."

Jimmy almost dropped his beer and Sachet's eyebrows bounced off his hairline. "What?!" shouted Jimmy, bending over to emphasize his words.

"I liked the idea of owning an island, so I bought one, but then I wanted another. At one point I had five all over the place, but I only kept the ones I really liked. Made a killing on them though. The market in the 90s was way down and the dot com bubble made a lot of money for a lot of people."

Nasser and Raj who were in the sitting area were now leaning in to listen and Mike felt he had to tell a story. He grabbed his beer and leaned back against the golf game. "I'm just saying, money has nothing to do with why I work, it never did. I truly enjoy programming. I don't care what language, what type of software or hardware. It's solving problems and it's logical. It just makes sense and it makes sense for me.

"I once asked a video game developer if he spent all his time coming up with new ideas and working on games. He told me 'No, this is just a job, do you spend every night programming?' He was so snarky. But my answer was 'Yes'. I mean you guys know this isn't all I do, but it's what I love and I program as much as I can. I know there's a lot of people in our industry now that do it because it pays well and it comes with a lottery ticket, but that's not me. Heck I let Gillian and Malcolm pay me in equity. I don't even take home a paycheck."

"Wow." said Raj. "That's amazing. I mean I like programming, and I know I work a lot, but I don't think I get the same out of it as you do. Although I always felt that way about school."

"I love what I do." chimed in Sachet. "I've always wanted to be a leader and now I have a team."

"Yeah," said Jimmy pointing his beer bottle top at Sachet, "but do you love what you do now, or do you love what your team is doing?"

"What do you mean?" asked Sachet.

"Are you sure being a leader is what you really wanted, or did you just think you had to move up the ladder? And now the people that work for you are doing your dream job."

"Oh. I see." Sachet looked thoughtful.

Mike replied, "That's why I never became a manager or a team lead, or anything. I like programming. Every company tries to move you up to leadership, why wouldn't you want more money? More responsibility? More power? But I don't want that, so I have never accepted any promotion."

"Don't get me wrong," continued Mike, "I love that I have the means to live like I do. I enjoy puttering on the arcade machines or bird watching on my islands, but if I had to make a choice, I'd sell it all in a heartbeat to keep programming." His face looked solemn and everyone in the room seemed to be deep in thought. "Ok, enough of the life talk, watch me kick Jimmy's ass." he said and moved out of the way.

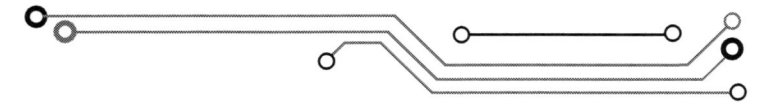

Milo was asleep in his van. The van was parked at McClures beach, about an hour and a half north of San Francisco. From the parking lot it was a short walk to the beach and it tended to be void of tourists and crowds. At night he would sneak out onto the beach and sleep to the sound of the waves rolling in, but it was still daylight and he had been working so much he wanted his makeshift bed.

His body wasn't used to the kind of drain it had been under with Dataffair skyrocketing. It had been his full time gig since January and most of it was spent training new PosiTechs and organizing schedules. He had booked this weekend off and already put in a requisition to hire a manager to handle all the paperwork. His plan was to do the training that he enjoyed and spend a few hours meditating and filling Anodes with positive energy. Organizing and planning was not his style and he could feel it burning him out.

This weekend with the beach, sun, and relaxing was exactly what he needed. It was awesome hanging out with the team from Waterloo. They were always interested in how they could make things better. Malcolm was flying in today as well, but that was a different story. Malcolm had been trying to write mantras and "programs" that he believed the PosiTechs could use to make themselves more positive. He didn't seem to get that the technicians didn't need motivation, they just needed to be themselves. Not that the notes hurt, they just weren't necessary. He rolled onto his back and stared at the van ceiling. He smiled remembering the last note. "I now prepare to tap the cosmic potential with an attitude of discovery, devotion and excitement". He might steal that one for his life coaching, he thought. "I am an independent piece of the Universal Mind" was another Malcolm had come up with. Well perhaps, "come up with" is the wrong term. Milo was pretty sure Malcolm was getting these from somewhere. Then he had created some kind of program that faded in these sayings on a large TV screen mounted to the wall while new-age music played. Milo was pretty sure Malcolm believed every problem could be solved with technology. He didn't seem to believe he was selling joy, he believed he was selling the technology to move joy around. He closed his eyes and began his breathing exercises to help him achieve sleep quickly.

He was woken up by Crosby, Stills and Nash singing "Teach Your Children" playing on his cell phone at 3:00 a.m. The screen sent a glow across the interior of the van and he shoved himself up and off the bed. It was Malcolm calling. He answered "Good morning boss."

"Milo! You need to get to the office right away. All the Anodes are empty and we are pumping negative energy to every customer."

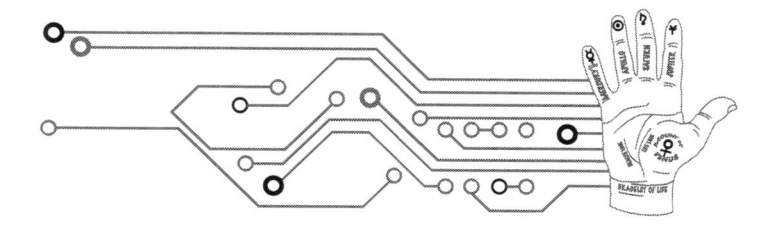

CHAPTER 0001 0000: THIS CANNOT BE GOOD

The Waterloo team were all in the San Francisco office. Packed into the Cosmic Positivity Center along with all the staff that belonged there. Dashiki were everywhere. Most of their wearers were lying down or sitting on cushions sipping tea. If you didn't know any better, you would think it was the trauma ward at a hospital. Jimmy was fetching tea and towels for PosiTechs that were moaning and holding their heads. Some were even crying, shaking with the weight of what they were attempting to do. The glass wall that showed the glowing Anodes was pulsing red as every single one was reporting zero positivity. Somewhere phones were ringing and the noise level of conversations and discussion made it impossible to hear the new age background music.

Malcolm had arrived at the office the night before, planning on taking a quick look around before retiring to his hotel. He was shocked to find the staff on call running around like their hair was on fire. Just after 9:00 p.m. the technicians on duty, which wasn't very many considering it was a weekend, began seeing the Anodes drain extremely quickly. They dutifully put on their psiPhones and attempted to recharge them. They found that the Anodes would not charge. The positivity just passed right through them. They had put an alert out to the R&D team assuming something was wrong with the displays. The Waterloo team had got the call and piled into a few Uber's to head over from Mike's house. By the time they got there more PosiTechs had arrived and were also attempting to fill the batteries. Nothing appeared to be working. Raj and Nasser had begun testing cables and Mike and Sachet were verifying that the Anodes were working. That was what Malcolm had walked into.

By three in the morning they had got nowhere. PosiTechs were burning out left and right. They would nap or meditate for a while and then go back to the psiPhones. Raj was now looking through all of their customers' dashboards and noticed not one was showing any positive energy at all. Malcolm didn't know who else to call, so he called Milo, surely he could give them some clue about all this cosmic, universal mind stuff that might cause a total drain of positivity. He had responded calmly that he was on his way and that made Malcolm feel better even if it was going to take two hours before he got there.

The Chicago office had gone down at one in the morning their time, which made it ten in San Francisco. The timing was odd, exactly one hour, thought Malcolm. Seattle and Miami were still operating as normal, something had to be going on. He went through the beaded curtain and found Raj sitting at Summer's desk. "Any word from the cable company?" he asked.

"Yeah, they say all their systems are nominal. And I've confirmed that energy is being emitted, so a signal is getting through, it's just all negative."

Malcolm sighed and rubbed his face. "It doesn't make any sense. Exactly an hour apart we lose two offices. The psiPhones are definitely working and I'm sure our people aren't the issue. I watched one woman totally drain herself with that stupid headband on."

"I don't get it." said Raj shaking his head. He wasn't sure what he was looking for in the system, but he kept looking.

The curtains were spread again as Jimmy came in. "What if we have some industrial espionage going on? One of these techs is actually pushing negative energy into the system."

"That wouldn't work," said Raj, still staring at his laptop screen.

"Why not?" Jimmy sounded agitated. It was late and everyone was getting to their last nerve.

"I modified the psiPhones back in April to just drop negative energy. I figured why even pass it on."

"What?!" cried Jimmy, "I didn't know about that change. Why didn't you just make all the emitters drop negative energy then? At least we wouldn't be spewing negativity everywhere."

"It's different!" said Raj, slamming his laptop shut. Malcolm jumped, but Jimmy just glared at Raj even harder. "You obviously forgot that there is always a constant amount of energy. So if we are emitting a signal and it's not positive, then it's negative. There can never be a void, there is always some type of energy."

"Well we could stop sending anything then. At least that's better than sending negative."

"Whoa whoa whoa" said Malcolm, throwing out his hands. "We need to work together here. Let's relax and think about it. If we stopped sending anything we'd be breaking all our service level agreements. Let's turn off a customer that usually shuts down for the weekend and see what the levels go to in that office. We can still monitor right? Even if we aren't emitting."

Raj opened his laptop. "We can do that."

"Based on our experiments, an empty room has even levels of

positive and negative energy," said Jimmy. "If we turn it off, we should see it go to half. Good idea."

The three watched as Raj logged in and turned off a single customer. He then flipped to a new tab and pulled up their dashboard. The little gas gauge style graphic had the needle pointing to 0 or empty. Completely negative. They watched and waited for a minute, silently urging the pixelated needle to move.

"Damnit!" shouted Jimmy. "What the fuck is going on?"

"This isn't us," moaned Raj. "Something is up. I'm turning off everything." He flipped to a terminal program and began typing in commands, logging into their system management node in the cloud.

Malcolm was stressed and looking far away. If they weren't the ones sending these levels, who was? And why?

"I'm shutting down the whole distribution system with your permission Malcolm." said Raj, two fingers hovering over the enter key on his laptop.

Malcolm sighed and pushed so hard on his glasses they slid up his forehead and broke. He stared at the pieces in his hand and threw them on the ground. "Do it." he sighed. "I'm going to have to start a press release. Keep looking and see if you can find what's going on. And get that cable company looking too, someone has to know what's happening."

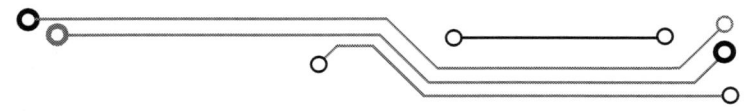

Jimmy turned and walked with Malcolm back into the CPC. Mike and Sachet were waving them over from the Anodes and they waded through the lounging and exhausted technicians.

"They just started charging!" said Sachet excitedly while Mike nodded. "It was out of the blue. There was nothing and then suddenly they were filling up, and fast."

"We know," said Jimmy sadly. "We've killed all the outgoing connections until we can figure this out."

"Oh," said Sachet. "Well that makes sense then. So the customers are basically back to zero?" he asked.

"No." said Malcolm, "We're still seeing 100% negative at our first test client."

Even Mike's eyebrows shot up at this news. "So even though we're not sending anything ... and if we were sending anything it'd be positive ... somehow the customer still has a negative level. That's an interesting problem."

"Yeah," stated Malcolm, "my understanding, and Jimmy can correct me if I'm wrong, is that not only is there a maximum amount of energy, it's a constant. So if there isn't positive energy coming through then the negative will just fill the void."

"Exactly." sighed Jimmy.

"Exactly!" said Mike, suddenly becoming very animated. "I got it." he shouted.

"Got what?" asked Jimmy, catching the enthusiasm. Malcolm noted Jimmy's sudden change in attitude, he was just frustrated a second ago and managed to turn it around with one display of enthusiasm.

"Someone is siphoning off positivity. Or I guess we could have a leak ..." Mike said, putting his hand to his chin.

"Oh!" said Sachet. "So the positive energy is being lost somewhere in the chain, obviously after the Anode since they are charging, but with the positive energy gone, the void is filled with negative energy."

"A leak doesn't make sense," said Jimmy. "Otherwise we'd be seeing the customers return to an even keel once we shut off the positive energy we're pushing. Someone must be actively pinching positivity out of the lines, so that there is a void."

"Oh yeah!" said Malcolm, now he was starting to feel the enthusiasm as well. "It's like a water leak, if the water pressure is turned off the water in the hose doesn't completely drain away it flows out the leak until the pressure is even on both sides. But if someone is sucking water out of the leak they can bleed that hose dry."

"Exactly what I mean." said Jimmy, slapping Malcolm on the back. Malcolm thought it was odd to be happy about one of his staff being proud of him, usually it was the other way around.

"So we're under attack." he said, realizing what it meant. Everyone looked around at each other, stunned as they thought about the implications of this statement. "DUDE! WHAT THE HELL?" Milo had arrived. He was standing in the middle of the room taking in the condition of his team.

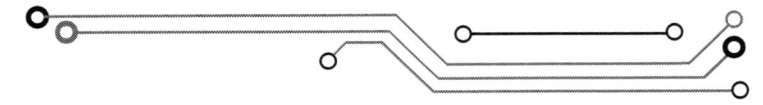

Milo went around the room like a triage nurse. He calmly removed any psiPhones he found still on heads. He checked on conditions and told many to get rest and relax. He opened the fridge and busted out a bunch of pre-made smoothies and began to hand them out. When he wasn't busy, his eyes glared at Malcolm. Once he had checked on everyone he calmly strode up to the group gathered by the Anode wall. Sachet and Mike excused themselves immediately and hurried into the sales area.

"What are you doing, man?" Milo started, obviously upset. "These are people, not your computers, you can't just push them harder to make your business work."

"Milo, I wasn't trying to overwhelm them." Malcolm didn't like confrontation. He tried to put on a stern face, he knew the CEO was where the buck stopped and he didn't want Jimmy to see him get reamed out.

"Well, you did!" Milo was standing perfectly still staring into Malcolm's eyes. "When your technology isn't working the way it should you can't somehow tap into people and drain the energy out of them."

"I was doing my job by making sure they did theirs."

"Your job!? Your job? That's all this has ever been to you isn't it. Make a ton of money ..."

"I don't care about the money." Malcolm quickly interjected.

"You don't care about the money? Then why are you doing this?" Milo threw his hands out.

"I'm creating a legacy, Milo. Building a great company, and these people are part of it. If all goes well they'll be telling their grandchildren that they were part of it, that they were there when it all started."

"No." said Milo, suddenly very calm. "If all goes well, they'll be telling their grandchildren they love them. They'll be eating ice cream together and talking about how blessed they are. They won't be talking about where they worked or how some corporation made them who they are. Dude, you don't even believe in all this!" Milo waved his arm around the room, from the Anodes to the technicians behind him. "I told you when we met, you need to be yourself. I don't think you heard me."

Milo was still staring into his eyes, Malcolm hadn't even seen him blink, and it was starting to agitate him in a weird way. "You're standing here now, a statue of Malcolm Joffrey, dressed up in clothes that you think are socially acceptable, attempting to live a dream that's not even yours. You bought your legacy dream from

TV and the media, and you're paying for it monthly with the rest of your life." Milo sighed and finally looked away. He's eyes surveyed the rest of the room. "Your legacy shouldn't be a company, man. What a waste of your life that would be. These people here are your legacy. They were your team, you were their leader. I'm taking them now. You need to get your head together and figure out who you are, because pretending to be a big-time CEO isn't working for you."

Milo didn't wait for a response. He turned and began to help the technicians up. He told them it was all over, that they should head home. Monday they could regroup and see what was happening.

Malcolm looked at Jimmy. He had that look people get when they wish they were anywhere else. "Well that was uncalled for." he said.

Jimmy looked back at him and stared at him for a while, then suddenly seemed to get a thought. "I don't know Malcolm. I think I was caught up too. Driving these people into exhaustion isn't how you solve a technical problem. Our own team wasn't the issue, it was someone out there." he pointed in a general outside direction. "We were all talking, yesterday I guess now ... that we do this job because we love it. But we all have other things as well, it's not everything, but it's what we enjoy. Why do you do it? I've always wondered that."

Malcolm stared at Jimmy, was this shit-on-Malcolm day, he'd have to check his calendar.

"I think Milo's right, you were never affected by the positivity, because you didn't believe in it. I think you need to figure out who you are. Maybe it is CEO, maybe it's something else, but you gotta be you." Jimmy walked over to the sales area and gathered up the rest of the team.

"We'll see you on Monday." Jimmy said as they left.

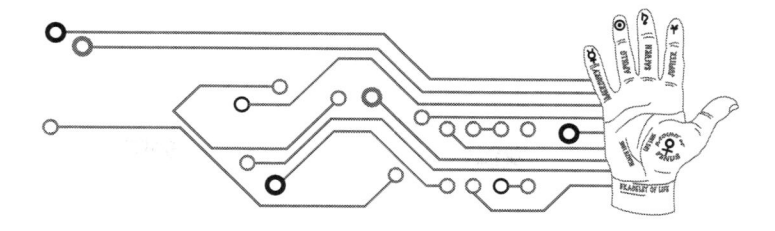

CHAPTER 0001 0001:
I WAS LOST

Malcolm arrived at his hotel at six on Sunday morning. He hadn't said a word to his Uber driver and only spoke to the clerk when necessary. He dumped his suitcase on the ground and flopped down on his back on the bed. He dug in his pocket and pulled out his cell phone. He was exhausted and beat. He scrolled through the numbers and punched Gillian's name. She answered cheerfully and bugged him about the time when she realized how early it would be on the west coast. He didn't hesitate and just explained everything that had happened, from the loss of all their positive energy, to pushing the PosiTechs and Milo's rant.

"Wow." she breathed. "That's a lot to take in."

"Yeah." he sighed. He stared at the ceiling for a while and neither of them spoke. "You know what?" he said, sitting up on the bed. "It pisses me off. The more successful I become, the more people want to tear me down. I mean even my own mother is constantly criticizing my choices. Oh sure, when she needs money for that loaf of bread she calls a dog, then I'm a good son, but when I'm doing great things, she thinks I'm wasting my time." He stood up and began pacing the room. "And Milo, who does he think he is? You and I built this company from nothing. I'm living a life everyone dreams of. This is what everyone wants!"

There was a pause as Malcolm caught his breath and he stared out the window. He could see the lights of the city below and a ghostly reflection of himself standing over the city. Larger than life, staring back at the small Malcolm stuck in the hotel room.

"Do they?" asked Gillian quietly. "When did you decide you wanted this legacy?"

"When?" Malcolm shook the giant image out of his head and closed the curtains. "What do you mean? I've always wanted to build a legacy."

"Really?" Gillian asked. "As a kid while everyone was playing house, you played boardroom?" she giggled.

Malcolm laughed too, his mood changing. "No. Of course not. I wanted to be a pilot. But those are childhood dreams, they aren't based in reality, I had a buddy that wanted to be an elephant when he grew up."

Now it was Gillian's turn to laugh. "So what do you really want to do now, assuming society wasn't going to judge you on it?" she asked.

Malcolm stared straight ahead, but he wasn't seeing anything, his mind was working. Was it possible he only wanted this dream because of outside influence? He thought about Elon Musk, Steve Jobs, and Bev Shepherd. Weren't they his heroes? Then he thought about Dennis Ritchie, Ken Thompson, Linus Torvalds, and Steve Wozniak, those were his real heroes. They were the computer programmers that truly created things. It was the difference between the doers, and the leaders. Maybe he didn't want to run everything, maybe he wanted to be the builder.

"I don't know," he said thoughtfully. "Maybe I just want to go back to coding ..."

"Well, it's good to hear you thinking about it. It's like Milo says, I know you don't want to hear about him right now, but you are trying to stray from the true Malcolm and I think that's why you're frustrated."

"Interesting."

"I think you are looking at things backwards. You are trying to start at the end with how history remembers you, worried about the people of the future and what they think of your life instead of the people around you right now and most importantly, what you think of your own life."

Malcolm began pacing again. "Well, that's all well and good, but it's not going to solve the problem we have come Monday when all these customers return to a negative atmosphere in their offices."

"True." said Gillian, "And I have some other news that at first was exciting, but may just add to your stress now ... " her voice trailed off as she spoke.

"Lay it on me," said Malcolm. "Think I'm pretty much at the bottom right now, not much could surprise me."

"Well Cheryl called me last night since you were on a plane. CNN wants to do a live special on Monday morning on the economic turn around in the US thanks to Dataffair ..." she sighed as she got it out.

"Oh my God." moaned Malcolm.

"Apparently the President is going to do a thank-you speech to us after." Gillian said quietly. "It was supposed to be good news ..."

"President of what?"

"The United States."

"Oh my God." repeated Malcolm and sat down on the bed. "I need sleep." he said and hung up. He flopped back on the bed and his mind shut down, completely overwhelmed. He was sleeping shortly after. His dreams were troubled with visions of the President of the United States telling him what a disaster he had created. He would be known as the biggest failure in history. Not exactly the legacy he was after.

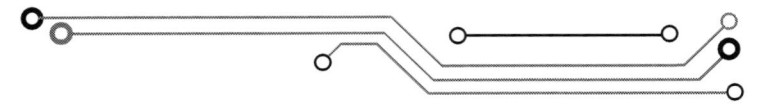

Sunday was a mess. Malcolm didn't wake up until the afternoon and he felt horrible. There were messages on his phone from just about everyone he knew except his team. Some had heard of the big interview and some had heard of the attack on Dataffair's systems. There was a missed call from Bev Shepherd. No message was left. He decided he would shower and then call her back.

The time in the shower was filled with thoughts about what to do the next day. They were going to stream him live from the hotel. Should he fess up to the disaster or try and play it off as a set back. Something they would overcome and push forward. By the time he was dressed he couldn't remember when he had showered. His body was moving without any intervention from his mind which was otherwise occupied. He kept ruminating the line "you never even believed in it" over and over again in his head. Something was there. That was the solution, he just needed the problem that fit.

He scrolled through the recent calls and punched Bev Shepherd's name. "Malcolm!" came an enthusiastic answer. "I tried to reach you earlier this morning."

"Yeah, I saw you called. I take it you heard the news?"

"Yes, Gillian filled me in on everything. Sounds like you are in a rough spot." There was no pity in her voice, just that same self confidence she always had.

"That I am," he said. "Do you have any great ideas?"

"Ha. No." Malcolm was surprised, he had been hoping for some sage wisdom from years of experience. "This isn't my problem. But I did call to give you some advice."

"Well I'd love to hear it." he moaned.

"Make your decision and stand by it. No one else is in your place, this is all you. You need to make the decision that is right for you and then you need to take action. Don't decide what to do based on society, or what the media will think, or how critics will judge you. Make the decision that feels right for you."

"Doesn't that go against the 'people are the solution' speech you gave us? Just do the right thing for me."

"No. And I'm not saying do the right thing for you, I'm saying do the thing that feels right. It's a big difference and I think you'll find that what feels right is also what's right for your people."

"Huh."

"Look, I gotta go, but I'll be watching tomorrow, heck, I may even record it. Either it will be a great example for my speaking engagements or it'll be a horrible example for my speaking engagements." She laughed and Malcolm didn't feel any better. "Good luck tomorrow. I know you'll do the right thing."

Malcolm hung up the phone. So much for the great business advice. He turned on the hotel TV which automatically tuned to a big Welcome screen advertising their room service and excellent swimming pool. He went to the on-screen guide and selected CNN. Perhaps something would happen to bump their segment, although he doubted it with the President appearing.

"... had come in to water the plants on a Sunday. Miss Tammy Daybal discovered a partner's wife, Mrs. Margaret Paget, already in watering the plants. A fight ensued in which Mrs. Paget was knocked unconscious. She is being treated on scene" Malcolm sat down on the end of the bed, only feet away from the large flat screen.

The shot was showing the Dataffair office building on Market St. There were police cars everywhere and the reporter was standing in front of police tape that blocked the entrance. "From police reports we know that Mr. Paget, hearing the commotion from his office called the police but at some point also wound up engaged in an altercation with Miss Daybal. It appears he was hit over the head with one of the planters and has now been rushed to the hospital and is considered in non-critical condition. Miss Daybal was apprehended by police while attempting to set fire to the office using the lens of Mr. Paget's glasses to focus the sun on some of the plants in the window. The Barton & Paget office has recently been in the news for their defence of the Tree That Owns Itself as well as their amazing story of positivity involving Dataffair." Malcolm's jaw had no muscles anymore, it hung open and his eyes stopped blinking, not really seeing, but just taking in what was on the screen. The broadcast cut back to someone in the studio.

"We will actually be having the founders of Dataffair on a special broadcast tomorrow morning Susan, perhaps they will be able to shed some light on this bizarre twist of events at the Barton & Paget office." Malcolm moaned and fell backwards onto the bed.

"Well Bob, their offices are right next door in this same building, so I'm sure they are well aware of this incident."

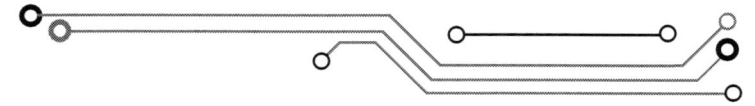

Matt called just after dinner San Francisco time. Malcolm had been staring at his TV all day. The news was full of Dataffair clients that had lost control. Some were just arguments that had escalated enough the media heard of them, things that would've been ignored on any other day. Some involved violence and the worst was in Seattle where police had arrested a man that had gone home and brought a gun back to the office. Matt sounded exhausted as he filled Malcolm in.

"So, we've all been explaining how to disconnect the emitter as clients call in, and Cheryl's team has been proactively leaving messages for any customers that we haven't heard from," he explained.

Malcolm didn't answer, still watching the TV on mute with subtitles turned on.

"Anyway," Matt continued. "I'm heading home. I don't know what to do about tomorrow, but I'm sure you'll think of something. I'll definitely be watching."

"Yeah." sighed Malcolm.

"Oh," said Matt as though he just thought of something. "I'd avoid the numbers. I know you like your stats, but I think this needs a more personal touch. Just be yourself, you'll do great."

"Thanks." said Malcolm without any enthusiasm as he hung up the phone. Just be yourself, seemed to be the mantra of the day he thought. Right now he'd like to be anyone else.

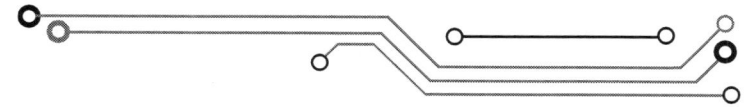

Malcolm barely slept that night. The images from the television running through his head. People got so angry, all because of a display that said the room was full of negative energy. He wondered if they had just programmed the displays to show positive and not bothered with the energy would it have worked just as well. And there'd be no way to hack them, they could've just made a static graphic that said "100% Positive". Maybe that's all motivational posters were. No, he thought, they tried to convince you to be positive. The Dataffair graphic had said you were positive, you didn't need convincing it was right there in front of you. And if you truly believed it, you were positive.

He looked at the clock, 3:33 a.m. He always liked that time. The witching hour some people called it. Suddenly he knew what he was going to say tomorrow. It hit him like a truck and he almost felt himself snap back to Milo's imaginary life line. His brain raced for a bit, but by four he was sound asleep and his mind was clear.

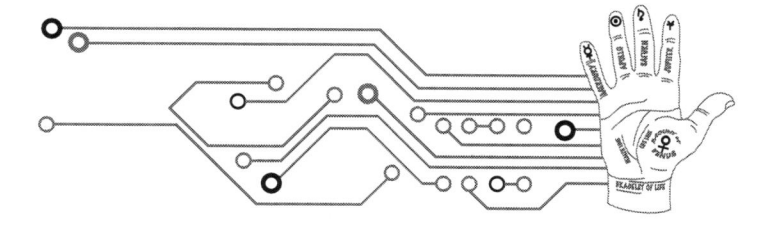

CHAPTER 0001 0010: END OF FILE

Malcolm was showered, dressed and full of caffeine by 5:30 a.m. The CNN interview was at 9:00 eastern time, so 6:00 here in San Francisco. The studio would be connecting to him via video chat 15 minutes early to make sure the connections were all good. Malcolm was dressed in a gray heather hoodie with University of Waterloo across the front and a pair of jeans. He gave up on his turtleneck style and in fact had put the ones he brought outside the hotel door for garbage pickup. Most of his suitcase was emptied except for the jeans and hoodie which he originally planned to wear if the team did some activity on Sunday where it was appropriate to dress down.

He made and drank two cups of coffee and was feeling ok considering he was running on an hour and a half of sleep. He pulled the hotel desk out from the wall and set up the laptop on it. The preview showed him sitting in a chair with a moderately attractive abstract piece of artwork behind him. He felt that the art was a perfect reflection of himself. Good enough for a hotel room, but mass produced and just too common to ever be recognized as great. He was ready for whatever came.

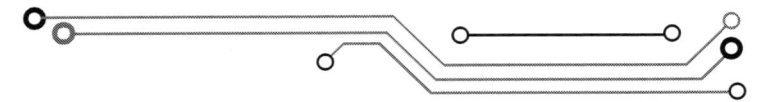

At 5:45 the computer started to ring and a window reported CNN was calling. He clicked the Accept button and sat back. Shortly two windows appeared on his screen, one had an empty CNN desk in it and the other had Gillian's face. She looked good, tanned and smiling. Her hair had been bleached out by the sun and she had a white tie front blouse on. She looked more relaxed than Malcolm had ever seen her and that was saying something.

"Good morning Malcolm!" she said cheerfully and waved into the camera.

"Good morning! It is good to see your face." he replied.

"You seem in good spirits."

"I am. I think I solved the cause." he said, winking.

Gillian smiled and her eyes went to slits. "That's good. I knew you would."

From somewhere a voice came on announcing they had 10 minutes until their host would join them. The CNN screen remained an empty desk, while the voice made sure they could hear them. They asked Gillian to close the curtains beside her and had Malcolm adjust his hood after asking if he was going to wear it for the interview. Malcolm felt oddly relaxed considering what he knew was about to happen.

As promised John Berman appeared at the desk with 5 minutes left to their live interview. "Hey guys," he said. "We're on a commercial break right now, but then I'll be talking about the events from the weekend and I'll introduce you. You won't be on screen until then, so if you need to check yourselves, do it before then."

"Sounds great," said Gillian.

"As a heads up, if the president calls in early, we'll be cutting the interview short. As you can imagine, his time is critical, so we don't want to hold him up."

"No worries," said Malcolm.

The two co-founders were muted and John began to talk about the last story. He led into the interview by talking about the events over the weekend. Malcolm made a face that reminded Gillian of a kid who had just accidentally broken a window with a baseball and she laughed. Soon John was onto the introductions and the two put on their serious faces.

".. the co-founders of Dataffair, Gillian Cliff and Malcolm Joffrey, good morning to you both." Malcolm saw his microphone come off mute.

"Good morning John," he said.

"It's a pleasure to be here," said Gillian.

"So, I'm sure it's been quite a roller coaster for the two of you and indeed, all of Dataffair, over the weekend." John began.

Gillian started, which was fine with Malcolm, he figured he'd be finishing. "It's been something. Even though I couldn't be at the office, I've been hearing about it non-stop." Malcolm appreciated that she didn't mention how she had stepped back. That would have been the reasonable thing to do, he thought, distance yourself from the problem. "This is the first psychic security event in the world and I'm glad we had the right team to deal with it."

"Yes," said John, "Now, you're calling it a psychic security event. What exactly does that mean?"

"The Dataffair psychic network was actively attacked by a malicious party," said Gillian. "We were targeted explicitly and the unknown actors were siphoning off all positive energy that the

Dataffair Positivity Technicians were producing."

"You actually have Positivity Technicians. Amazing. Before this attack Dataffair was on top of the world, your clients have been in the news constantly over the last few months with just an unbelievable amount of innovation and productivity. I think it makes sense that we start with that, the positive, if you will. Can you tell us how Dataffair made these clients so successful at what they do, Malcolm?"

Malcolm put his hands on his thighs. This was it. "Absolutely." he said as he leaned forward. "We place a digital dashboard in the customers office, like you might have in your car, except it's just a digital representation. And like your car dashboard, we have various gauges and lights that come on and tell you what's going on."

"I understand." nodded John on his screen.

"If we move the positivity needle to 100% and the people in the office believe it, then they are more positive. And when they are more positive they produce better, they start to be themselves and relax. They stop trying to be machines and doing what they think needs to be done and they start doing what they know needs to be done."

"Wait?" said John, obviously picking up the subtlety that Malcolm hadn't said they actually made them positive. "Are you saying there is no positive energy?" Malcolm could see that Gillian was attempting to hold her smile, but had no idea what was going on.

"I'm not saying there is no positive energy. I'm just saying that we aren't sending it. You don't need Positivity Technicians or PositiviTV to be positive. You just have to believe in yourself."

"Wait, wait, I'm sorry. This is total news to me. Are you attempting to say the whole thing is a hoax?"

"No it's not a hoax at all. If you believe in it, then it works. We didn't change those people. We just made them believe that they had no reason to be negative. It helped them remove their fear, especially knowing that everyone they were dealing with was also believing in them."

"Wow! People believing in themselves is great, but why did people believe you?" John asked, incredulous.

"Because we had technology. We put up a big TV screen and displayed charts and gauges on it. We installed a device that we said was emitting positivity. People believe in technology more than they believe in themselves. I even asked my home assistant the other day what 20% of 100 was. People have learned that technology can do anything, so when we told them it was making them happy and productive, they became happy and productive."

Gillian's jaw dropped, she had given up on her facade.

"I'll tell you this John," Malcolm continued, "and this is the important part. The things those people did, the good things, that was all them. They have the real power to change who they are. We can't pump positivity into their lives, but they can, and they can share it with others, just like they were doing. Each one of those people were creating positivity, that's how it works."

John was flabbergasted, "But Malcolm, the obvious question then, if you had control of the gauges, why would you let them go negative like they did on the weekend, knowing how people believed in this technology?"

"We didn't. Here's the thing John, I'm the only one at Dataffair that knew we were sending out white noise and calling it positivity. If my staff didn't believe in the service, they wouldn't be able to pass on their beliefs to anyone else. So when these malicious actors took our signal, the gauges just did what gauges do, they showed empty.

In hindsight, it would've been better to lock them at 100% positive.

"The critical part here, John, is that it was the people in the office that created the positivity. Those people did it! They started creating again, they started innovating. It was no longer a job, but a passion and that's why they changed. They didn't need our technology, but the technology made it seem easy to be positive. And if you believe it's easy, you do it.

"I want all the viewers to know, you can be more positive and engaged. You don't need us, you just need to be yourself. Good luck everyone, I hope each of you changes the world."

"I'm getting news in my ear, probably not a huge surprise, but the President won't be able to make our call today."

Malcolm looked at Gillian's image on his laptop, she was smiling and nodding. She knew it was all over.

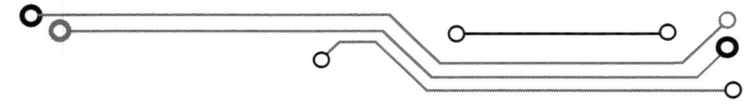

Six months later, Malcolm was sitting in another office. The company was a small startup that had just got their seed funding. It was called Blue Glue and they were going to be writing a new comprehensive security system for enterprise corporations. The office had been painted blues and grays and there were family photos everywhere. The door opened and two women walked in. They were dressed like they had biked to work and were young enough Malcolm wondered if they had bothered to graduate. The second woman was pushing an office chair into the room.

"Malcolm!" said the first, "It's a pleasure to meet you. I'm sure this interview is just a formality based on what Nasser and Jimmy have said about you." She took a seat across the desk from Malcolm and her partner pushed her chair in beside her.

"I have to know," said the other leaning in, "Did they always fight about desserts like that?"

Malcolm laughed, "Yes, always." he replied.

The two ladies watched him for a bit, but when he didn't continue they resumed.

"Well this position is for a senior developer, but there is definitely going to be room to move up."

"That's OK," said Malcolm, "I don't plan on moving anywhere, I just want to code."

"Awesome. That seems to be a thing these days. The corporate ladder is getting a bad name. I totally understand." She started taking notes on her laptop.

"Hey, I've been wanting to know since that Dataffair fiasco ... no offence." started the other.

"None taken." smiled Malcolm.

"Was it really all lies? Or were you guys able to transmit positive energy? Jimmy and Nasser won't talk."

"And we've tried." laughed the other woman.

Malcolm smiled and looked around. "Is that your son?" he said pointing to a digital picture frame on the window ledge.

"Yes, it is." said the first woman.

"Then it was all true."

ABOUT THE AUTHOR

Kenneth Roland grew up in St. Catharines, Ontario, Canada, where the 'lake' is north and nothing is south. He has an older sister and a younger brother all from the same biological parents.

He attended Westdale Public School where he wasn't really known for anything except attendance, and his mom was mostly responsible for that. He graduated to West Park Secondary School where he met his first IBM clone and fell in love.

For quite some time he attended Niagara College Tertiary School taking Computer Engineering Technology, but that was mostly because he really enjoyed playing pool.

He skipped Quaternary School and went straight to work.

He has worked at a newspaper, a pre-press shop, a real estate company and an exclusive audio-video manufacturer. He ran his own company for 7 years after breaking a mirror.

Kenneth participates in the Ludum Dare game competition under the pseudonym 'Doc Kaos' and can be found on Twitter @DocKaotic.

He now lives in Kitchener, with his wife Rebecca, 2 of their four girls and a cat. An oversized pug is also permitted on the property.

He didn't write this book to make a lot of money, and so far at least, that's working out.

Manufactured by Amazon.ca
Bolton, ON